WELCOME
to the
LAST RESORT

"We offer incomparable services—of every kind.
Food, alcohol, sex, drugs," Stone's guide recited
in bored tones. "Gambling rooms are on levels
17–20, drinking and drug rooms, 15 and 16, sex
and orgy rooms are on 10–14. The death games
run from 5–9, and the standard sports and
recreations are on main floor to fourth. Girls,
boys and transsexuals can be ordered at any time
for private pleasure in your own rooms. Merely
pick up the phone by your bed and specify your
request. Please have sex, age, and other vital
information ready when placing your order."

Suddenly Stone tripped on the curved walkway.
While the guide waited impatiently, he looked
down and started. It was a body, a woman—
naked and covered with blood on her face and
chest. She had been mutilated, horribly...

* * *

ALSO BY CRAIG SARGENT

The Last Ranger
The Savage Stronghold

Published By
POPULAR LIBRARY

THE MADMAN'S MANSION

CRAIG SARGENT

POPULAR LIBRARY

An Imprint of Warner Books, Inc.

A Warner Communications Company

POPULAR LIBRARY EDITION

Copyright © 1986 by Warner Books, Inc.
All rights reserved.

Popular Library® is a registered trademark of
Warner Books, Inc.

Cover art by Norm Eastman
Cover design by Rolf Erickson

Popular Library books are published by
Warner Books, Inc.
666 Fifth Avenue
New York, N.Y. 10103

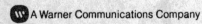 A Warner Communications Company

Printed in the United States of America

First Printing: December, 1986

10 9 8 7 6 5 4 3 2 1

CHAPTER
One

MARTIN STONE looked into the black hole at the business end of a 12-gauge sawed-off shotgun and said good-bye to the planet Earth and his ass, not necessarily in that order. The barrel pressed hard against his face, covering the tip of his nose so it was actually sticking inside the muzzle. Stone knew that if he breathed hard, the damned thing was going to go off, splattering his brains from here to New Mexico (not that he particularly gave a fuck where they landed—just that they wouldn't be in his head anymore).

Another, and then another cold barrel pressed in on him until he could feel nearly half a dozen pistols and rifles covering him from every side, all of them held by black-leather-jacketed Guardians of Hell with scarred, toothless, boil-riddled faces that one didn't want to look at twice. And all of them were just aching to pull the triggers of their bloodletters. Stone wanted to raise his hand to touch his neck, which felt like it was nearly broken and wet with blood, but he didn't. He cursed himself for not having been more alert. He had been riding in moonlit darkness on a backcountry road heading north through western Colorado when— He must have run into something—a trap of some kind. There had been sudden, brain-jarring pain, and then he was on the ground, gagging.

"Well, what have we caught here?" the voice attached to the shotgun poking between his eyes laughed, making the freezing metal barrel grind around Stone's face a few times, leaving a trail of purple bruises behind. Stone knew the slime at the other end of the 12-gauge—he was part of the Pueblo gang, the one they called Scalper because of his habit of taking the top of a man's head off with a hunting knife after he killed them—and sometimes before. Stone glanced for just a second at the man's motorcycle, parked several yards off in the semidarkness—the handlebars covered with human scalps, dangling beneath the metal horns like hairy banners of death.

"I think we caught us that scum who took out Straight, not to mention our whole fucking scene back in Pueblo," another voice spat out from behind Stone. He turned to look, but the butt of a .45 slammed into the side of his skull, making him see black and then a galaxy of dancing white stars flying around his head.

"Don't move, asshole, or you're dead!" a gruff voice piped through the fog of pain.

"Why, I do think you're right." Scalper laughed again. "I think it is Mr. Stone. Why, this must just be our lucky day. Just the luckiest day we've ever had. You see that? We throw up a nylon rope across this road here just to see what kind of goodies we can snag, and lo and behold—we snag us what we want more than anything in this whole fucking world. The good Lord doth provide for them what provides for thems-selves." He crossed himself mockingly with the blade of a long bayonet that he held in his other hand.

"Yeah, this is our luckiest day, Stone," said a huge, bearded face, suddenly looming into Martin's view as he came back to full consciousness from the gun blow. "And it's your unluckiest!" From out of nowhere a fist the size of a football, with metal rings on every finger, slammed into Stone's face like a cannonball, crunching bone and sending him back into the dancing galaxies again, only this time the stars were crying tears of blood. From out of the swamp of burning darkness Stone could hear them talking and feel them tying his hands, then his feet, together tightly with leather thongs. The cold of the snow and ice on the ground woke him quickly, and his senses came on just in time to hear a motorcycle start up several feet away.

He had barely opened his eyes, to see a cotton swab of a moon staring back down from the sky, when the Guardian bike shot forward on the snow-covered road. Stone felt himself suddenly jerked forward, trailing behind the roaring motorcycle as he bounced up and down on the cutting ice like a sled made of flesh. He wasn't in the mood for this, wasn't in the fucking mood at all, Stone thought absurdly as he flew down the road on his back at thirty miles an hour. Some nights a man wouldn't mind dying—some he'd even welcome it, but tonight Martin Stone was too damned tired and disgusted to head off into that cesspool of used souls they called death. Not that anybody gave a damn about his feelings being hurt—not when his body was about to be torn into long, fine shreds that could be served in a Chinese restaurant—if there were such things anymore.

"Shit," Stone spat out from between his rattling teeth, which cracked against one another as if they might be thinking of taking a leave of absence from his mouth. "Shit, shit, shit," he screamed into the air with a kind of madness, though none heard him above the roar of Scalper's motorcycle dragging him as the other bikers followed behind whopping and laughing as they occasionally let off a shot or two that dug deep holes in the snow around him.

He had to clear his mind. Somehow. But the sheer bumping, the weight of the earth slamming into him again and again as he flew wildly along the one-lane road, made it almost impossible to think. It was like being in an earthquake, an earthquake that wouldn't let go. He could feel the thick leather on the back of his jacket starting to rip and tear from the abrasive sandpaper of the cutting ice below. In seconds it would cut through—and then the frozen shards and the rocks would turn his back into badly ground hamburger and his spine into something that resembled a broken umbrella.

Suddenly he hit a large bump in the road and instantly was flipped over onto his front side so that his face was flying by half an inch above the blur of ice below, his jacketed stomach bouncing along like a stone skipping on a pond. He forced his elbows out with all his strength, forming a sort of protective grid just in front of his face. Every few seconds one of the arms would strike something and it hurt like hell, but at least his eyes were protected—

4

for the moment. For the moment—he almost laughed. He only had a few moments; this wasn't exactly your two-month chess-game kind of deal where you had twelve hours to make a move, think I'll go home, call you in the morning. This was mutilation, followed by bloody death within seconds.

What the hell would the Major have done? he wondered fleetingly. But Stone knew with growing horror that the Major couldn't have done anything—and neither could he. There was no way out. He couldn't move his hands, which were stretched far out ahead of him, dragging the weight of his entire body. He thought he still had the Uzi, but there was no way in hell to reach it. The pistol might as well have been a million miles away, though it was strapped to his chest, only feet from his bleeding fingers. The thought finally filled his fully alert consciousness that he really was going to die. There was no way out. He didn't feel fear. Just . . . sadness, that he wouldn't be able to help his sister, April, who he had saved from marriage to the leader of the Pueblo Guardians of Hell just two days before, taking out most of the city along with them. He had thought he had killed them all, but he was wrong. These bastards had survived. And he would die, and she would die—if she was lucky.

He hadn't really realized that he believed in God until that moment. But somewhere inside him he mouthed a silent prayer as if to say, "ready a bed, a mattress would be fine, don't go to any trouble—but I'm coming up real soon." He hit a sudden drop in the road, and on the upswing his face dug into a little crust of hard ice that ripped long tracks down his flesh, just missing his eyes. The ice claws tore from scalp to jaw, each long gouge instantly dripping blood, leaving a trail behind him in the white snow. His eyes filled with the salty liquid so that he couldn't even see for a second—just feel the pounding of the road against his chest and stomach so he could hardly breathe, and the spray of ice churned up from the motorcycle's wheels, spitting into his mouth and nose. It was all over but the dying.

CHAPTER
Two

THE SPEEDING blur of the world suddenly slowed and then stopped, and Stone came to a skidding halt, his body tumbling end over end on the ice-coated road as Scalper turned his big machine around on a dime and came up alongside his victim. He looked down at the bloodied, half-conscious, snow-caked thing that stared back up at him, somehow still defiant, and grinned with a smile that came all the way from hell.

"Still alive?" The bearded face laughed. "That's good, that's real good. Maybe we can keep this thing up all night. I ain't had this much fun since I raped me a pair of twins up in Dakota. I'll just go back and forth on this nice scenic stretch of road here until you're snake chow." With that he turned forward in the seat and began to twist the accelerator. "See you down below, asshole" were his friendly parting words. With that he threw the big BMW into gear, and it lurched forward like an elephant out of the starting gate.

It got five feet. Out of nowhere a shape hurtled through

the air from the dark bushes along the side of the road. Stone, his eyes closed to protect them against the icy shrapnel he knew was about to start shooting up at him again, heard a scream and a loud, crunching sound, as of a coconut being cracked in half. Then the bike fell over and skidded sideways along the slick surface, dragging Stone behind it about ten yards until it came to a grinding halt against a scrawny pine tree. Stone sat up in a flash and looked back. The biker was down, his head split into two distinct pieces. Even from twenty yards off Stone could see the bright red that covered the man's face and neck, and the pink brain stuff bubbling out from all sides of the cracked skull cavity.

And standing atop the corpse's chest was Excaliber, his pit bull and traveling companion. Stone had left the animal in the camp he'd set up to spend the night and had just been scouting ahead when the Guardians caught him. But the bull terrier, all ninety pounds of murderous muscle, had sensed something, disobeyed his orders, and traveled three miles through pitch-black woods to find him.

The dog trotted jauntily over toward Stone, its muzzle painted bright red, and stopped a few feet away, looking at him with a quizzical, somewhat mocking expression as it turned its head sideways, as if to ask how he had gotten himself into such a compromising situation.

"Stop posing for the cover of *Dog World* Magazine for Christ's sake," Stone yelled, working frantically at the leather thongs that bound his hands as the bouncing headlights of the other bikes, which had fallen behind, were rapidly approaching around a bend in the road some seventy-five feet away.

He held his arms out in front of him, pulling the wrists as far apart as possible. "Here, bite!" he said, presenting the leather binding to the dog. "Bite, bite, bite!" The bull terrier looked straight into his eyes, as if making sure that was what Stone really wanted, and then, angling its head sideways so as not to break the flesh, it managed to push its furry, triangular-shaped head between his arms and get some teeth around the leather. It bit down hard, seemed to chew the thongs around for a few seconds, and then spat them out, stepping back. The deer-hide bindings fell free from Stone's hands.

He reached down, whipping out his custom bowie and in a flash sliced through the bindings around his ankles. He jumped to a crouch pulling out his Uzi 9-mm machine pistol from its jacket holster, slammed a thirty-round magazine into the bottom, and then quickly screwed on the four-inch-long silencer. Checking to make sure that the approaching bikers still couldn't quite see him, Stone ran forward in a crouch, moving like a shadow himself through the wide, weaving shadows of the trees, the full moon flashing intermittently from the churning sky of clouds above.

"Here dog, down, down." He called for Excaliber to get out of a patch of moonlit ground, blazing as if it were on fire, and the animal shot forward toward him, covering the ten yards in seconds. It hid alongside him behind the still slowly spinning wheel of the dead biker's motorcycle. There were five of them left, Stone knew as he waited for them to come in full view from over a rise. But they thought he was dead. Surprise, that was what Major Clayton R. Stone, his late father, had always stressed. With surprise—a man could do almost anything.

The bikes roared toward him, the five lights piercing the darkness like spotlights, searching to illuminate a scene of death.

"Yeah, there he is," a voice yelled out from the lead bike. "Look's like Scalper's already done gone and killed the asshole. Must be washing off the scalp." He laughed. The laugh stopped in mid-release as the first three of Stone's silenced 9-mm's caught the thin, weasel neck in one-inch spacings around the Adam's apple. The biker threw his needle-scarred hands to his throat as he gurgled out a flood of blood from each of the holes. He fell face forward from the bike as the handlebars suddenly turned on their own and the motorcycle flipped over, slamming into the ice, cracking his face into mush. The bike skidded around sideways and into the path of the two Guardians right behind it. One of them managed to avoid the debris, but the other slammed into it and went flying from the top of his bike, soaring like a wingless bird through the air right toward Martin Stone.

Stone raised the Uzi just for a second, to make sure the flying slime wouldn't somehow crawl back to consciousness and try to get him from behind. Two quick shots slapped into its fat stomach, and the thing landed with a bloody thud yards behind him. But Stone was already firing forward again, taking out one more, with a stream of five slugs that scissored down his face, cutting a line from forehead to chin that seemed to just open up and spew out everything within it—eyeballs, brain tissue, tongue, and teeth—into a bubbling stew of parts in the road, a steaming smorgasbord just inches from the gushing corpse that dove forward into the white snow.

But it wasn't going to be that easy. The remaining two bikers had already submerged in the shadows that grew thicker as the moon seemed to faint away in the sky, and everything suddenly went coal-mine black and starkly silent. Still, he was doing a hell of a lot better than he'd been doing about sixty seconds before, Stone thought, trying to encourage himself as he crawled combat-style straight away from the bike towards the grassy knoll on the side of the road. Not a moment too soon as a spinning steel ball spiraled up through the frigid black air like a badly thrown football, and came down right on top of the bike where Stone had been just seconds before.

The World War II grenade exploded, sending the Guardian motorcycle into a roaring geyser of steel and fire, as tongues of flame licked out, igniting the little rivers of gasoline that swept off in every direction. Three other bikes lying nearby on their sides were inundated by the fast-burning wave of fire, and their gas tanks ignited simultaneously, sending up a roar that shook the ground Stone lay on. One of the remaining Guardians was crouched behind his bike, but the flames found him. The river of fire flowed beneath him and roared up into his crotch and chest. Instantly the Guardian's thick, greasy beard popped into flame, followed by his shirt and then the black hair on his head. The screaming biker leapt up from his hiding place and ran through the night, a fiery inferno of human flesh, his testicles blazing like furnaces, his face completely yellow with licking flames dancing over his eyes and mouth, blackening everything they touched.

Stone didn't bother to waste ammo on that one, as the blinded biker rushed off into the woods, a candle of human wax flickering off to its own hellish death in the frozen forests. But there was still one more. Stone glanced around trying to spot the damned dog, but it was nowhere in sight. He looked back with a pounding heart at the fiery bike he had been shooting from a minute before, but he could see nothing but the blazing metal pickup sticks that were left.

Suddenly he heard the sound of cracking twigs. He rolled over on his back just as a shotgun released a 12-gauge load of bone-smashing shot. The charge dug out a hole in the ground big enough to bury a bowling ball just inches from his head. Stone know weapons well enough to know that the thing was a pump and that the biker as about to fire again. He didn't have time to stop and aim, so Stone just continued the roll and swerved off at a sharp angle so as to change direction. The shotgun blasted again, sounding as if it were just above his head. Stone felt a sharp sensation in his left shoulder and arm, and then total numbness. The Uzi he had been cradling in that hand fell free as he slammed into the dismembered handlebars of one of the burning bikes.

Stone whipped his head around just in time to see the gargantuan biker standing over him, the huge shotgun aimed right at his heart. They both heard a growl at the same instant, and the biker turned to see its source. The pit bull flew like a striking snake through the air, its jaws opened wide, ready to clamp down on the man's throat. But the biker was fast. He swung the pump around and let loose with a shuddering blast. The charge caught Excaliber in the forward left shoulder, sending him back spiraling backward into the snow as if he'd been kicked by a mule.

But it gave Stone two precious seconds. He twisted his head and saw a jagged sliver of metal about five feet long, burning at the far end. Reaching around with his still functioning right arm, Stone grabbed hold of the spear-shaped scrap and winced as the heat of the metal instantly burned his palm, raising little blisters of red. But there wasn't time to find anything else. Stone sat up and spun his body, swinging the flaming remains of one of the bikes up toward the Guardian of Hell who was himself turning back from blasting the bull terrier.

"Bastard," the Guardian screamed from between black-toothed lips. "Die, you motherfucker! Die now!" He pumped the spent shell clean, and his finger reached for the trigger that would send Stone into the worm business. But the finger never tightened. Stone's jagged, but razor-edged, sword flew into the biker's throat, slicing straight through it for a depth of about five inches. With the neck virtually severed, the head, no longer held up by anything, slowly leaned backward and then fell from the red, bubbling stump that once had been home. The bloody ball started toward the ground, but with a main artery and part of the vocal cords still attached to it, like wires to a dangling light-bulb fixture, the head stopped falling after about six inches and swung back and forth against the wide black-leather jacket.

Somehow the biker stayed on his feet, for what to Stone seemed like minutes. Actually it was just eight seconds. Just stood, like a statue in the snow, the gun still aimed, the legs still spread, everything as it had been in life—only without a head, without a trace of life left in the husk of humanity. Then, with a sudden gust of wind from down the mountain road, the thing lost balance and toppled forward into the snow, the neck gushing out a flood of thick, red liquid into the pristine white, dyeing the surface around it for yards with a slowly spreading purple stain.

Stone rose with a groan, looking at his left arm and shoulder. It was bad. Blood was oozing out everywhere. But it was still there; he couldn't feel any bones poking through. Not really wanting to, and with just about the heaviest heart he had ever carried within his chest, Stone half hobbled over to Excaliber, who lay off in the shadows. There was no way the dog could have survived. Not with a blast like that. No way; the damned thing was dead by now. In his mind he prepared himself for the worst, vowing to bury the goddamned animal right then and there even though his arm felt like it was on fire.

But no canine services would be conducted that night. As he approached, Stone heard a low growl and then saw the pit bull trying to right itself in the darkness, splattered with its own blood, as if it had been wading in it.

If it was in any kind of pain, the animal didn't seem to know about it. But then its kind had been bred for centuries not just for their incredible fighting abilities but also for their toughness and their resistance to pain. And Excaliber's was one of the toughest of the blood lines—Red Dragon.

As if not even wanting Stone to know it had been hurt, the pit bull somehow regained its balance, scampering up onto its three working legs and stood there; the fourth, the front left leg, which it held several inches off the ground, was absolutely coated from paw to shoulder in red. But the damned dog was alive. And so was he.

"Pal, I owe you so many fucking dog biscuits now," Stone said, stumbling back toward his own bike as the pit bull hobbled along by his side, "I think I've lost count. So let's just even it off and say—a crate, okay?"

Excaliber looked up and barked, his almond eyes bright with the excitement of the evening's fun and games. The animal had been bred to kill tigers. Fighting a half dozen killer bikers had just gotten its juices flowing.

CHAPTER
Three

S TONE AND the pit bull walked over the remains of the bodies that littered the charnal ground on the back-country road as the burning bikes continued to blaze like bonfires on all sides of them. The snows that were coming would bury everything until the next spring. No one would ever know just what had happened here. Don't leave a calling card, the Major had told him. Whatever you do, wherever you go—appear and disappear like a shadow, never leaving a clue of your existence.

Stone mounted his huge Harley 1200 Electraglide and turned the ignition. With its automatic electric start the black machine roared instantly to life, vibrating fiercely beneath him like a bull ready to crash through a fence. Excaliber jumped up onto the long, wide seat behind him and latched his back legs around the leather padding; his forward, working leg as well. Stone knew the dog usually clasped the padded seat with all four paws, like a starfish around a clam, but the three would have to do for now. The animal was strong as an ox. Stone wasn't going to worry about him. Besides, he had enough worrying to do on his own—like driving an immense motorcycle, the size of a small car, with one arm through the snow at midnight. And just to add some icing on the cake of imminent disaster, Stone felt himself growing dizzy from the loss of blood from the shotgun blast to his upper arm and shoulder. He didn't even want to look at it. He'd tied a tourniquet around the upper arm; there was nothing else to do but hang on and pray.

Stone eased back on the throttle, and the Harley jerked ahead on the icy surface, nearly pulling the right handlebar out from his one good arm. The other he placed on top of the left bar, a useless piece of meat without the slightest bit of sensation down to his fingers. No problem, Stone thought darkly, he'd just teach the dog to do surgery, and between them they could reattach his severed muscles and nerves or whatever the hell had been done by the biker's blast.

He left the headlight of the bike off so as not to be seen. There could be more bastards out there. Whichever of the Guardians had survived the recent purge of their ranks by Stone and the resistance fighters of Pueblo had obviously just hightailed it on out to the hills to pick up their former vocations of mountain bandits and murderers before they had gone career-minded and become high-class drug-dealing extortionist killer bikers. And with his luck—the fellows he'd just met had been the nice ones.

Stone knew he had no choice but to head straight for the mountain base just north of Estes National Park, in the northern part of Colorado where he had been living for the last five years with his father, mother, and sister, of whom only his sister, April, was still alive—for how long he had no idea. Stone could hardly begin to imagine what Poet, the quadriplegic dwarf and his mini-army who had kidnapped April and taken her to his armed fortress/retreat in Vernal, Utah, would do to her. The hideous, egg-shaped psychotic was capable of anything. But Stone wasn't much of a threat to anybody with one arm himself. April would have to hold on for at least a day or two. And somehow Stone would have to make it to his hidden mountain shelter. At least there were medicines and antibiotics there for him and the dog—and he wouldn't have to worry if something would scalp or eat him if he passed out for a day or two.

With nothing to lose but his life, Stone set himself as comfortably as he could on the Harley's leather seat and tore ass straight up the center of Colorado. He knew he had almost two hundred miles to go—and there was no way in hell he was going to make it. But that was the idea. He welcomed the frigid air biting against his face, slapping him awake from the dizziness his lost blood had created. The red stuff wasn't exactly sloshing out of him, but it was doing something. Every time he looked around he could see that his entire side was covered in blood. Even the side of the bike and his pants had streaks of red paint running along them like racing stripes.

"Come on, come on," Stone exhorted the motorcycle as it roared through the dark night, the moon but a sliver on the horizon as little pockets of glistening silver snowflakes fell from time to time. Hour after hour he drove forward, never stopping, hardly moving, turning from time to time to see how the pit bull was doing, but the animal seemed to have gone into some sort of momentary hibernation and appeared to be sound asleep, all of its working legs gripping tightly to the side.

"That's it, doze off, dog. You sleep while I drive," Stone muttered incomprehensibly into the wind, trying to keep himself awake through conversations with himself.

"So, how you doing pal?" Stone asked as the bike came to the foot of a steep mountain road that disappeared in fog banks ahead. Granite monoliths towered above him, rising forever into the rushing clouds.

"Not too good, pal," Stone answered back. "Not too good at all."

"And why is that?" Martin Stone asked himself, snapping his head up as he suddenly realized it had almost been touching the handlebars.

"That—is because I don't think I know where I am, who I am, what I'm doing, or where I'm going," Stone snapped back.

"That's all?" Stone asked sarcastically.

"That's all," Stone replied sullenly.

"Then drive on, asshole. That's the lamest excuse I ever heard in my goddamned life," Stone commanded.

"Yes, sir," Stone snapped back, coming to attention so that for the first time in hours he was actually sitting upright on the bike. They were going up what seemed like the ninety-degree side of a mountain, and he could hardly see a foot ahead of him. Between the blood-draining dizziness that swept over him in waves now threatening to topple him from the bike and the thick, moist, freezing fog that kept almost turning to snow, Stone knew he was in big trouble.

Even in the midst of his half-unconscious confusion he was fairly sure he was heading over Vail Pass—and that meant that the slightest mistake would send him hurtling over a thousand-foot-plus drop—smashed to ant pâté before he could scream.

The image of being squashed in such an ignominious way sent a bolt of fear and repulsion through his veins, and a surge of adrenaline followed along right behind it. His mind suddenly felt clearer than it had for hours. As he reached the summit the snow thickened and began swirling around him, and Stone felt his face and cheeks start to go numb as the huge, heavy flakes came flying almost straight at him. He pulled the visor of his helmet down over his face, but it quickly smeared and he couldn't see a thing. He flipped it up again and surged forward into the blizzard.

The thick, nearly impenetrable snow lasted a good hour, with Stone edging forward slowly, at only about ten miles an hour, not in the mood to tempt the fates. But soon he could feel that they were heading in a downward angle, and the snows seemed to slacken. Suddenly they were out of the white curtains completely, and the night around them was sparkling, crystal clear, like a picture postcard. Stone could see half of Colorado below him spreading off in every direction as the very tip of the red-faced morning sun started to crawl into view to the east, like a bloated all-night drinker searching for a grassy bed to fall into. Somehow Martin Stone knew he was going to make it . . . at least this time.

It was virtually downhill for the next fifty miles, and then a long, fairly flat stretch all on still drivable, albeit weed-blanketed, roads. With the sun clear and bright and no one making a sudden leap from behind one of the myriad rusting car wrecks that littered the road, Stone made excellent time. At last he exited the Interstate and headed down a one-lane asphalt (or what had once been asphalt) road for about eight miles until he saw the sign, three steel posts side by side, that signaled the way to the mountain shelter.

Without stopping, Stone wheeled the whining bike through the thick brush covering the start of the road. Good—it looked as if no one had been through here. What little road there was, was overgrown with brambles and weeds. It appeared more of a deer trail than anything man had ever made or used, which was just the way his father had planned it. Even bandits would think there could be little of value at the end of such a wretched, bramble-strewn passage. Stone had to move slowly as the crowding brush and over-hanging branches grew thicker. But after a mile or so they thinned out again. Feeling he'd just made a journey that had lasted a lifetime, though he'd actually been on the road for just thirteen hours, Stone at last made the final turn in the road and there it was—the Bunker, in all its dead glory. He pulled up and stopped the bike, dismounting as the auto kickstand flipped down. The pit bull awoke itself from its sleep, yawned, and looked at Stone to see if the journey was in fact over, or if he was just relieving himself by the side of the road.

"Yeah, we're here, mutt." Stone grinned as he saw the animal's sleepy eyes and its obvious reluctance to move if it didn't have to. "Come on, get down," he said softly, suddenly feeling a burst of affection for the animal that had already saved his ass at least five times in the last two weeks.

"You'll like it inside. Got chairs to chew on, things to break—and dog biscuits—or something even better, I promise you." With so many alleged treats being offered it, the bull terrier could hardly refuse and snapped its narrow eyes open, jumping down onto the snow-covered ground and landing with perfect balance on just three operational legs.

Stone had left the radio transmitter that opened the solid rock wall of the hidden shelter beneath a boulder off to one side of the entrance. The rock weighed over three hundred pounds—to make sure that neither man nor animal was ever tempted to move it. He put all his weight against the oval boulder and, pushing with his entire body, managed to slide the thing aside. The transmitter was there, sealed in a plastic wrapping to protect it from moisture. He slipped it from the plastic and walked over until he was standing directly in front of what seemed to be the impenetrable rock face of a mountain that rose above the plateau he was standing on for another two thousand feet. Stone pushed the "open" button. And let out a deep sigh of relief, for the green, lichen-covered rock parted as cleanly as if split by a logger's ax and, humming softly, slid into shafts on either side. Pushing the bike, Stone, with the pit bull by his heels, walked inside, both of them looking around cautiously, all senses on alert.

It felt weird to be inside again. It would always feel weird. Everything was changed now. His mother and father were dead, his sister . . . They had all lived here as family for years. From the moment his father, Major Clayton Stone, had awakened in the middle of the night and had known something was wrong and made them rise and pack and ready to leave within twenty minutes from their Denver house. That night they had driven forever, too, and he'd been right, for the bombs had begun going off far in the distance at the very moment they reached the mountain base hewn into the sheer rock face that the Major had had constructed over the last two years. And there they had lived together, the four of them for five years, without once setting foot outside. Sometimes hating each other, sometimes not— but always so close, right on top of each other, even with over fifteen thousand square feet of living and work space.

He felt their presence all around him. The spirits of another age, an age that would never return, moving through the dark shadows of the dimly lit garage like creatures made of the darkest matter, the molecules of nightmares. The huge stone door's mechanism suddenly clicked loudly and the four-foot-thick solid sheets of rock slid automatically closed, timed to do so after twenty seconds unless the "open" button was hit a second time.

The lights flicked on automatically as he entered the inner chambers. Electric eyes had been mounted everywhere so that lights were actually activated only when someone was passing through or present in a room—one of the Major's many energy-saving devices. The place still looked just as it had when they'd all left it. Suitcases half packed, clothes strewn around the couches and the thick rugs in the living room. Jesus, had it only been a few weeks since he'd emerged into the hell that was now America in this post-nuke world?

The plan had been to just scout around for a few days— but that's not how it had worked out. To say the least. Stone quickly glanced around the place to see if any problems had sprung up. The thermostat controls seemed to have functioned perfectly in the absence of human fiddling over the last three weeks since he'd been there. The Major had always sworn that the mountain-blasted shelter could continue to care for itself—cleansing and purifying the air, monitoring all electrical circuits and plumbing systems by computer, able to shut them down if anything went wrong. The life-support system even watered the plants throughout the bunker automatically and would do so for ten, even twenty years, on its own. Martin had his doubts. But then the odds were that he wasn't going to be around to see the final results. The damned watering devices would probably outlive him.

He made his way to the kitchen and pulled a few cans of canned chicken down from a shelf.

"Here, dog," Stone said, opening them with the electric can opener that stood just to the side of the glistening stainless-steel sink. "This is just an appetizer, so don't start getting all disappointed now. I promised you a feast—and a feast you shall get. So just chaw on these while I find a new shoulder, okay?" Excaliber's eyes suddenly looked more alert than they had for days, and the filthy, blood-coated animal licked its lips as the thick, sweet smells of the chicken, in oil, wafted down to it. Its wet, black nose opened and closed like a vacuum cleaner. Stone placed the plateful of four cans of the stuff down on the floor and pulled his hand away in a wink as the ravenous pit bull let out a lusty growl and tore into the meal face-first.

Stone headed toward the shower, taking off his clothes

as he walked down the plastic-tiled hallway, just throwing them where they fell. He stepped into the bathroom, and the lights came gently on. He turned the faucet to the wide, sunken tub, and water shot down from the shower head, instantly steaming hot from the solar-heating panels camouflaged in the features of the mountain above. The hot water quickly cleansed off all the outer layers of blood, and Stone got a good look for the first time at the wounds he had received. It wasn't as bad as he had thought. The blood came mostly from a lot of fractured veins rather than anything major. His skin was peppered with little craters where the shot had entered in. And Stone knew what he was going to have to do next, though the thought of it made him nearly want to puke.

He totally cleaned every part of the wound, and sitting on the edge of the tub, he swabbed the shoulder and upper arm down with alcohol and then took the scalpel he'd taken from the cabinet, part of the Bunker's medical equipment, and began digging in searching for the lead pellets that had taken up residence in his flesh. Actually cutting into his own skin hurt like the blazes, since he knew where he was going to cut and was already waiting when it came.

But the first slice is always the hardest, and once he struck pay dirt and pulled out a shot with a pair of tweezers, letting it fall to the marble floor with a tiny clang, he felt more confident and set out in earnest after the other pieces of metal lodged within. He knew that infection could start almost immediately and that once he passed out, he might crash for days.

But the concept, as always, was easier than its implementation. He found himself growing dizzy again, as weak as if he had no blood left at all. Swaying back and forth on the edge of the tub, Stone forced his eyes to focus and pushed the narrow scalpel into another little bloody hole, fishing for metal. It took nearly half an hour, every second his nervous system threatening to send him toppling, but at last Stone had the last of them out. He stood up somehow, washed the sheen of blood that had recoated his side, and then poured the whole bottle of alcohol over everything. There were bandages galore in the walk-in closet, filled floor to ceiling with every kind of medical equipment as well as a number of drugs. His father had planned every aspect of the place with all the zest of a true paranoid— trying to plan for absolutely every eventuality. And his paranoia had proven to be absolute reality. Stone found vials containing antibiotics and also penicillin. Figuring two microbe-fighting armies were better than one, he swallowed a few tablets from each.

Carrying a few supplies under his arm, Stone staggered down the hallway stark naked, drops of blood occasionally falling, but not nearly as much as before. He reached the kitchen, again nearly fainted, but kept himself standing. He had one more task to perform—and then he could fall into sweet unconsciousness, could sleep in safety for as long as he wanted. Excaliber was sitting by his bowl, looking down at it as if he were praying it might sprout more of the taste treat he had just experienced. For the pit bull had been taken with a sudden and most powerful love of canned Hormel chicken. Its mouth began salivating the moment it saw Stone, and the canine whined, pointing its muzzle toward the shelf, knowing there were more cans up there.

"I swear you'd take a bite out of death himself if he got too close." Stone laughed and then stopped just as quickly as the sounds made his shoulder move and sudden fiery pains lanced through it.

"All right, first the patching up, then the food," Stone said firmly, dropping, almost falling, to one knee. He washed the dog off, first with water, then alcohol, and as the grit and grime of its own dried blood came off, Stone saw that the dog had been lucky as hell. The shot had done a lot of damage—nearly a square foot of the animal's side was ripped away, but it had come sideways, so mostly surface layers of fur and outer muscle sheaths had been destroyed. The blast had richocheted off the animal's chest, literally sending it flying. The area was red and raw and still oozing a thin, watery blood. Stone smeared an antibacterial salve over every square inch of the wound and then surgically taped a large piece of cotton webbing over it.

"At last," Stone said, standing up and surveying the medical treatment he had wrought. He couldn't help but burst into laughter again, ignoring the slices of torture that shot down every nerve, for the fighting pit bull, toughest canine ever bred by man, looked quite ridiculous in the diapers that stretched clear around its stomach and chest and up onto its back. If the animal had had the slightest streak of narcissism, it would have suffered terminal humiliation at that instant, for its reflection could be seen clearly in the shining, waxed, black-tile floor of the kitchen. But the dog was far more interested in the culinary delights it had been promised than its image and got up on two legs, putting its paws on Stone's stomach as it pressed forward with all its weight as if to say, "Pay up pal, it's time."

"Dog, I know you think I've been shooting my mouth off the last few weeks about all these rewards of food for your saving my ass so many times. And I'm sure that in that dog mind of yours you were thinking this guy's just another asshole who's not going to deliver. Well, tonight," Stone said, pulling up the cupboard drawers above him with a dramatic flourish, "I'm going to show you—you're wrong." He looked up at the rows of canned food piled high and randomly began reaching up and taking down whatever his hand landed on.

"Tonight we're both going to eat until we drop." He took five of the cans and opened them on the electric wall opener, quickly sloshing the contents out into bowls that he grabbed from the china shelf. Canned chicken slid into one, peaches into another. Then tuna fish, olives, and goose pâté. Stone lowered the bowls as fast as he could to the floor and then reached up for more cans, not even looking this time at what he grabbed. The pit bull's eyes grew wider and wider as it sniffed at each new gourmet delight. It had never smelled so many foods at once and hardly knew how to deal with the situation. It found the canned chicken and gobbled that down in a few seconds. Then it went from bowl to bowl, taking deep licks of the contents to see what it fancied. The peaches it pushed away with its nose, but the tuna it licked to the last scrap, then the dog swallowed a dozen sour pickles and the juice within to wash it all down.

Stone was moving as fast as he could now as cans of spaghetti and meatballs, corn kernels, red cherries in syrup, and a jar of mayonnaise all were opened and handed down. The dog was caught somewhere between ecstasy and nervous breakdown. It turned and turned in circles, its nose so inundated with scents that it could hardly tell what was meat and what pure sugar. Deciding that ultimately it didn't matter, the ninety pounds of pure muscle just closed its eyes, the heavy secondary defensive lids flapping down for protection, and dug in. Its tongue slapped in and out like a conveyor belt as the pit bull began sweeping everything in sight into its ravenous gullet, blind to what was coming in. Cherries, pie crusts, puddings, Spam, mustard, olive oil, meatballs, all were taken by the sandpaper tongue, swept up, and swallowed whole.

Still Stone kept piling the stuff down, in a state of near madness and exhaustion. His eyes were half closed, and his legs trembling wildly like overplucked rubber bands. He hardly knew where he was, just mumbling over and over, "Owe you? My ass, dog. Eat everything in the place. Eat, eat it all." Suddenly he stopped dead in his tracks and his eyes just closed, closed and wouldn't open again. His body had had enough, whatever strange games his brain felt like engaging in. Stone headed forward, like an old tree whose roots have finally just given way, and landed sideways, crashing down right into a dozen or so overflowing bowls of the canned feast. He was asleep, out cold before he hit, and instantly fell deep into terrible dreams. Nightmares in which the dwarf chased him in its electric wheelchair, firing from the machine guns in each armrest. Chased him everywhere so there was nowhere Stone could hide, and he was as naked as the day he was born, without a weapon to his name, and his feet kept slipping in something, in mud—or blood.

As Martin Stone dreamed on, pedaling his feet in puddles of apricot syrup, the bull terrier continued to lick at the bowls that had been set around it on the floor, continued to eat everything in sight. For it knew, as do all animals, that one eats what one can get. And eats it fast.

CHAPTER
Four

WHEN STONE awoke, he didn't know whether to laugh or cry. He was lying in an immense, pungently odored swamp of spoiled food. He sat up and felt with disgust how sticky his legs and back were. And then he saw the dog, its stomach pushed out to twice its normal length, like a python that had swallowed a cow, lying flat on its side under the kitchen table, breathing heavily with its mouth open as it tried to digest the immense load it had taken in. Well, Stone had carried out his promise. Whatever happened, the dog could never fault him on that.

Stone pushed himself up and looked at the clock. It read 10:17. He had slept for nearly thirteen hours. No wonder he felt so hungry, he thought, his stomach growling like a wolf. Suddenly he realized that he had raised himself up with both arms. His arm was working again. It hurt like hell, but he could feel every part of it. *He could move it!* He turned his head sharply to the side and saw that the little craters of flesh from which he had extracted the shot were already scabbing over, not even oozing anymore. So they were both going to live, whether they felt like it or not, Stone thought as he headed back to the shower to rid himself of his gravy and fruit-syrup coating. Unless, of course, the damned dog died of a burst intestine.

After his shower Stone walked through the house wearing just a towel around his waist, leaving a small trail of water on the floors and carpets. His mother would have raised a storm, but it was his place now—for better or worse he would do as he felt. He made his way to his room and took out a set of cleanly folded clothes—a pair of jeans and a black sweater. He still felt not so much tired but aching. He'd taken a hell of a beating over the last few days. His stomach growled again and this time didn't stop, so he made his way to the kitchen, and after cleaning up the remnants of the previous night's bacchanalian festivities, he made himself a real breakfast of powdered eggs, canned bacon, and homemade frozen bread, all cooked in the microwave oven in just under sixty seconds. He ate it all and then had seconds.

Glancing down under the table, he heard a slurping sound and saw Excaliber's puffed face poke out from beneath the round dining table. But the pit bull took one look at the steaming food, rolled its eyes back in its head, and then disappeared again into the semidarkness, like a turtle into its shell, not to reappear for hours.

After the food and two cups of coffee Stone headed down the long hallway to the back part of the complex where his father had built his "special room." None of them had been allowed to go into it, not for the entire five years they had lived in the bunker. The Major had spent half his life in there, trying to justify it all by saying he was experimenting, trying to build more devices for the shelter, things that would benefit all of them.

Martin walked to the steel door that stood at the deepest sector of the mountain fortress and waved his palm in front of the electric eye that streamed back and forth. Nothing happened.

"Damn, I forgot," he muttered out loud. He bent over and punched in a combination on a touch-sensitive keypad. The solid door of steel slid open with barely a whisper on its Teflon-coated runners.

It was like a mad scientist's workshop inside, with tables cluttered with oddly shaped devices of every conceivable description filling the lab. Stone walked across the twenty-five-by-sixty-foot work space, looking all around at the flashing lights, the video monitors that read out streams of numbers relating to information that the Major had preset the devices to measure months before; charts of outside temperatures, radiation readings, air moisture, and a dozen other things Stone couldn't even understand. And all of it powered by a central computer that kept the whole ball game running, kept everything carrying out its function even when there was no one taking the data down, no one who cared anymore.

At the far end of the room stood the high-tech lab's main computer, an immense device with keyboard and screen set on a Formica-topped table, and four crate-sized plastic boxes filled with circuit boards that sat atop one another on each side of it. With the superminiaturization his father had been experimenting with, Stone knew the thing must have the memory of a super-computer. He flicked the monster machine on and then pushed "enter." He had discovered the computer when he had broken into the room upon returning to the shelter after his parent's death. Unknown to him, his father had left a legacy of digital information for Martin Stone. His flesh gone, the Major had found a way to continue to try to influence Martin's life even after death. Martin had to hand it to the bastard—he got what he wanted, one way or another.

The advanced model IBM XT chugged a few times as electrons flowed through it, snapping it into life. Bright green digitally formated words scrolled up onto the screen. Martin couldn't resist but bring up his father's words, the ones he had read just weeks before, a voice from the grave.

"If you're reading this, it most likely means that I'm already dead. It also means that you've found out that the world outside is not as I told you. This will doubtless just add fuel to your fire of thinking me a manipulative, tyrannical old man who couldn't bear the idea of people deciding things for themselves. And who knows—there's probably some truth in it. But that's not why, in my own heart, I did it. At first I thought of telling you all that the bombs hadn't destroyed everything, but when I listened over the shortwave in the months afterward, I heard a radio chronology of the breakdown of a civilization as people described the savagery that was erupting all around them. I heard the screams come over the air as people were hacked to death while begging for help over their transmitters. Screams that hurt my eardrums sometimes, they were so loud. And so I decided, for better or worse, to keep us all in here until things had worked their way out, until the worst of the beasts had destroyed one another. And I would do it again. There's life out there, Martin, but none of it worth meeting.

"When the Nuke War started, each side launched tremendous quantities of missiles, though only a dozen or so actually got in. There was one thing all the theoreticians hadn't counted on—the EMPs. Electro-magnetic pulses put out by the first wave filled the atmosphere with so much electric garbage, created such a shield of interference that the rest either detonated high in the stratosphere or fell harmlessly into oceans and forests. But all communications equipment, TV, radio, phones, and much of the power supply of both American and Russia were knocked out.

"Then the European Military Coalition and the Third World Alliance stepped in—they'd had enough. And who could blame them? Between us, America and Russia had come close to adding another dead planet to the solar system—just what it needed. Using only conventional weapons, the EMC and the TWA invaded in an armada of ships and planes that made D-day look like an excursion. And when it was all over, virtually all of both superpowers' military capabilities and remaining nukes had been destroyed. Never again would either nation be able to threaten the world. The Euro-Armies withdrew leaving the U.S. in a state of virtual quarantine with land mines, nets, and battleships surrounding her every side so that she could not wreak her murderous nature on the rest of mankind. The same was done to the Soviets.

"After that it was downhill in a wagon for us over here.

There were countless mutinies, uprisings in what remained of the military and the CIA. Everyone wanted to rule—and so none of them did. The president and Congress were finally forced to flee the Capitol as angry mobs of tens of thousands stormed the place demanding food, medicine, uncontaminated water. None of them has been heard from since. Over four years.

"With my radio equipment I was able to get a general picture of what was evolving. At the very beginning it wasn't so bad. People tried to cope, tried to remain human to one another. But as the remaining stocks of food and fuel grew scarce, they began turning on one another, fighting like dogs over scraps. Once again things were decided by guns and knives. And as always happens as society reverts to barbarism, the meanest, the cruelest, those who could kill and intimidate better than the rest rose to the top. Within one year America had deteriorated into a dark ages not unlike the Early Middle Ages. Plagues, pestilences as murderous as anything mentioned in the bible, hit the U.S. And each city, each little town became its own walled-off society, superstitious, afraid, and extremely violent toward anyone who came and tried to take what little was theirs.

"I kept hoping it would get better, Martin. Prayed that it would. I vowed that as soon as the reports I heard over the radio grew even a little brighter—as soon as I heard that there were at least pockets of humanity trying to rise—we would leave this place. But those words never came—instead, only pleadings for help, people begging for someone to come and save them from the warlords, the murderers, the cannibals that were upon them. Then even the radio transmissions grew less and less, until there were only a few.

"Things are bad out there. From some of the transmissions I heard, bad beyond belief, bad even beyond the living hells I experienced in my years as a Ranger and in Special Forces. I'm sorry, Martin. Sorry that I had to do it all the way I did, sorry that you and I never communicated the way I had always hoped we would, that we somehow always disappointed each another. Sorry for the whole rotten world you and your sister were born into. At any rate, I can only assume that you will be going out there. And were I you, I would do the same. Be wary, Martin. I've taught you much in the ways of destruction. You'll need every bit of it. I wish I could have taught you more, but as you remember, there was great resistance from you at certain times.

"I've spent much of these last years, when I was holed up in here, putting down everything I know on computer. If you need it, it's here. Every bit of data I possess on warfare, fighting, siege, espionage, and every other goddamned thing a man could want to know on how to kill another man is in here. In this computer. Should you ever want to use it, just type in 'Directory' and press 'enter.' The subjects are broken down alphabetically from A to Z.

"This probably all sounds pretty bizarre to you—and doubtless confirms your belief that your old man went over the edge at the end. But I just want to end this computerized postmortem with a final thought—and then, if you don't want to, you'll never have to hear from me again for the rest of your life.

"You never asked me why I was a soldier for all those

years. And I never volunteered the information. But I'll tell you now. It sounds corny, Martin, but it was to defend freedom. And particularly the freedom of the little guy not to be stepped on by the bastards of this world. I made a lot of mistakes along the way as did my country, but for me it was something I had to do. A man ultimately is alone, Martin, completely alone. Whoever you share your life with—they may be inches away—still we are born alone, live that way, and sink back into the ground on our own. And what you do must be decided by you and only you. The kind of person you want to be. The side you choose in the ongoing struggle of good and evil that man carries with him through history like a cancerous growth on his soul. And the odd thing is—no one really cares what you think or do. Only yourself. But you know. You know deep inside, and every action defines you in terms of the light or the darkness. Every action makes you more of a man— or something else. Something without a heart, a soul. Something that preys on its fellowman like wolves on a carcass.

"I was a Ranger, Martin. That was my self-definition. Liberate the oppressed. I taught you what I knew so that you might carry on the battle—might carry the flame. Might be the—Last Ranger, the last son-of-a-bitch dumb enough to care what happens to those around you. It's your choice, son. God be with you. And know that whatever you think of me, in my heart I always loved you and did what I thought was right."

The words ended and the screen went blank for a second and then returned to Main Directory. Stone just stared up at the monitor as if paralyzed, his mind in another world.

It filled him with such mixed emotions to see those words, those thoughts of the Major's. They had fought each other in life, two willpowers that could not admit submission to the other. And yet . . . And yet the old man had been right about just about everything Stone had accused him of being wrong about. The world out there was terrible. Far worse than even his father could have imagined. Just Martin's few weeks outside the shelter had seemed like a lifetime. And the Major had been right about Martin's need to know about killing and the art of destruction.

All his life he had denied his father's philosophy, had fought hard to resist it—yet now, more than anything else, that was exactly what he needed to know: how to fight, how to take on a whole goddamned fortress single-handedly. Because, from what one of the top Guardians of Pueblo had said, before he had been relieved of his brains and throat by one of the revenge-seeking townsfolk, the headquarters where the Dwarf had taken April was virtually impregnable, perhaps the most protected structure in America. And the dwarf himself, the zen koan Poet of violence, was taking on more significance in some larger scheme of things that Stone was only just beginning to see. Rather than just isolated gangs of psychos, there was a pattern to it all, a structure emerging as to who actually ran things in postnuke America. But Martin had a long way to go before he could even start to put the pieces together. And he doubted he was going to live long enough to finish the puzzle.

Not really knowing what the Dwarf's fortress retreat was like or how big it was, Stone just went right to SMALL FORCE ATTACKING FORTIFIED STRUCTURE OVER 1,000 MEN on the menu. He pressed "enter" and waited for the battle instructions to appear that his father had keyed into the machine long ago. Yeah, that sounded about right, one against a thousand. If it turned out to be even worse than that, it hardly mattered, didn't it? He was so over his head already, another thousand men or two, a few battle cannons were hardly things to quibble over.

"Give up! Turn around and walk away!" the top line of the screen read out in brilliant green letters. Old Dad, always the card. Stone groaned, shaking his head from side to side though he couldn't stop the grin that swept his face. This grave-to-life communication was a little weird. Stone swore he could feel his father's presence in the room, standing over his shoulder, encouraging him to use all that the Major had left for him. But this spirit seemed friendly, not repulsive like the worm-crawling, maggot-infested ghost-father who had appeared to him in his peyote visions with the Ute Indians, who had saved Stone from death.

"If for some reason you must attack," the monitor read as Stone kept slowly scrolling the text up line by line, "Then your only chances are: 1) surprise, 2) explosives. A small force attacking a well-fortified position that has artillery is in the worst of tactical situations with every negative on his side, and every positive on the enemy's side. However, there are ways around this:

"1) Attack the fort, not the men. Your enemy is irrelevant, at least initially. Your basic objective should be to destroy the structure that protects the enemy along with their biggest weapons. After that, amidst confusion, loss of chain of command, and negation of their heavy firepower, you can move in and effect elimination of troops.

"2) Use of explosives. Explosives, placed in just the right places, can take down anything! The whole point in warfare is to use technology to your advantage—and negate the enemy's advantage. It is a chess game, Martin, where the stakes are life and death, and you have tenths of a second to make each move.

"Kinds of explosives..."

Martin read through the nearly fifteen pages of instructions, filled with writing, charts, blueprints of typical fortress structures, and every other damned thing that fifty years of experience had taught Major Clayton R. Stone, one of the toughest sons of bitches who had ever walked the face of the earth. And if Martin was to survive, he would have to be even tougher. The instructions were thorough and practical, and after going through them twice and taking some notes on a small notepad, Stone felt he had absorbed as much as he could. A lot of it might be very helpful. He'd have to see. But as he had no Einsteinian ideas of his own as to how to proceed, he would use what was offered.

He set the computer back to menu and then turned it off. It was time to go. He was functioning again, his arm was moving—and April was waiting. Stone stood up and with a funny look on his face, threw a mock salute to the still fading green letters on the dark screen.

"Thanks, Dad," he whispered. "Though to tell you the truth, I think I'll be seeing you pretty soon." He walked back through the rectangular lab and didn't touch a thing, not one of the beeping, throbbing machines that filled the

41

shelves. If they wanted to keep chugging, let them. They were his father's toys. Stone hadn't the foggiest idea in hell what they did, let alone how to turn them off. He closed the thick steel door so the lock clicked solidly and then headed down the hall to the munitions room.

Inside, the steel shelving units that ran along every wall from floor to ceiling were filled with a virtual armory of modern weapons. Rifles of every caliber, automatic weapons, pistols from .22s all the way up to huge magnums, ground-to-air missile launchers filled the olive-green shelves of the concrete-walled room. Major had planned for every eventuality. There were enough goddamned weapons here to launch a private army. The only problem—ammunition. A large shipment had been scheduled to arrive the day after the A-bombs landed. It never showed. There was plenty for the moment—enough to last Stone awhile, anyway, though he seemed to be expending a lot of it lately.

Martin had had heavy hands-on experience in the firing of everything from an automatic machine pistol to a tripod-mounted 50-caliber heavy machine gun—along with every other weapon that could take off a man's head or spill his guts. He and the Major had taken constant firing practice on the granite range at the rear of the mountain shelter, a long, narrow cave that had never been equipped for living. In the five years they had been in the bunker, between the two of them they had blasted far into the hard rock, digging nearly ten feet straight backward. And Martin had discovered that certain weapons seemed to suit him perfectly, that he could move fast with them and with deadly efficiency.

He reached up and took down a box containing a Ruger

.44 magnum Redhawk with stainless-steel body. He had lost the other one in the collapse of a church in Pueblo, which had taken out a good fifty Guardians along with the gun. But he wanted another one. He felt naked without it. The thirteen-and-a-half-inch-long Ruger with its integral base system—barrel recessed to accept scope mount—fitted with Leupold 5X scope with floating red sight dot was accurate to over a hundred yards, amazing stats for a handgun.

He strapped the reassuring weight of his quick-draw holster onto his right hip and then took down boxes of shells in their quickload applicators. He also pulled out several dozen thirty- and fifty-round magazines for his Uzi 9-mm autopistol. Then he walked to another shelf and grabbed five boxes of 12-gauge shells for the Browning BPS that sat on the side of his Harley.

He hauled the load of deadly supplies through the house and out to the front chamber where three cars and his motorcycle stood side by side, the automobiles covered in plastic tarps, fueled and ready to go. Stone stacked the ammo in sealed black plastic cases on the back of the bike, then headed instantly back for more—more minirockets for the Luchaire 89-mm rocket launcher that was attached on ball-bearing brackets to the side of the Electraglide. He had used up all six of them in just weeks. What had seemed like an inexhaustible supply of the sixteen-inch rockets just days ago had been barely enough firepower to keep him alive.

Still he needed more. The biggest mistake he could make would be to underestimate the bastards. He headed back and filled the biggest of his supply boxes with dozens of packets of plastique—little slabs of what looked like gray dough in cigarette-box shapes—until it was so full, he could hardly lift the damned thing. But he carried it out and set it on the back of the motorcycle. The big machine sank an inch but took the weight easily on its super-torque suspension system. That was it. The bike couldn't carry another bullet. It would do. It would have to.

CHAPTER
Five

"COME ON, dog, you better to be able to move." Stone scowled as he stood by the kitchen door, staring at the moaning animal that didn't look like it wanted to do any moving at all. It lay on its side, barely managing to raise its head, and stared up at Stone through pleading, half-opened eyes.

"You ate it—now you have to live with it," Stone said unsympathetically. "Stay if you want, I don't care, I'm leaving," he said, and turned, heading straight toward the garage. The dog looked after him for a few miserable seconds and then, knowing that he meant business, the pit bull groaned and flipped itself up on its side with all its strength. Its stomach was huge, virtually dragging to the ground. It belched loudly several times and started forward, moving at a slow pace as it followed behind its master.

Stone mounted the bike, and the dog somehow pulled itself up, wrapped itself around the thick, soft padding, and quickly fell asleep again or acted as if it were. Stone opened the rock door with the transmitter and they were out. The sun was as bright as a flashbulb as he rode slowly on the purring Harley. His eyes had adapted to the much lower light level inside, and now he squinted hard, as they actually hurt from the streaming swords of starlight. He stopped the bike and stepped off as the autokickstand swung down, balancing the machine before it had shifted an inch. Stone wrapped the radio transmitter back up in the plastic and placed it carefully down in the hole, pushing the three-hundred-pound boulder back over it. He kicked around the bottom so the brown, weed-strewn ground looked undisturbed.

Stone remounted the Harley, took one long last look at the mountain wall behind which his whole past lay buried as if in a crypt, and wondered if he'd ever see it all again. Then he turned and faced forward, letting the full weight of his body press down on the leather seat and hit the accelerator at full throttle. The bike roared forward, actually going back on one wheel for about thirty feet, making the dog whine unhappily from the back. But Stone settled the huge Harley down and eased her to a crawl as they headed back along the brush-covered dirt road to the world and whatever hell awaited them this time out.

He made excellent time, heading due west on the back roads of western Colorado, roaring through the sun-dappled afternoon with the warm wind flying against his face in kissing caresses. It was almost as if everything were all right, almost as if it were all before the war and he was out for a Sunday spin. Almost. But not quite. The rusting carcasses of cars and trucks along the two-laner gave evidence of a different tale. A tale of radiation poisoning and disease and God knew what ill. The skeletons of the original inhabitants of many o. ...e vehicles were still in them, or lying around them in pieces. They had all been stripped as clean as ivory tusks by crows and rats and ants, by maggots and millipedes that had chewed every square inch of edible tissue from them until there was just bone left—hard, uneatable bone. And the bones had become shiny from the months of sun beating down on them, the rays forging them into grotesque sculptures of death that smiled back at him through broken windshields, their bony hands in some cases even gripping the half-twisted wheel, as if steering right into the other world. Glancing through one smashed-in hulk of steel, Stone saw two pairs of skeletons face-to-face, arms wrapped tightly around each other. It looked as if they had been making love when they left their earthly bodies behind them, fused together unto death, never do us part.

His backbone rippled with a sudden shudder, as if he shouldn't be staring too closely into the world of the dead. He might see too far. It gave Stone the creeps whenever he passed these cemeteries of the highway. But they were everywhere. The vehicles had been stripped of all their usable parts or wiring so that they were skeletons, only rusting frames. And within them—the skeletons of the human dead still sitting where they were at moment of expiration, undisturbed. No one had use for a dead man's bones. Not even in post-nuke America.

They'll last a thousand fucking years, Stone thought as he shot through the obstacle course of extinct cars and people, monuments to the best that Western civilization had been able to aspire to. He kept his eyes from wandering into each little domestic scene of death and just concentrated on the towering forests of pines and the mountains that stretched out all around. Without the dead the Rockies were beautiful this time of year.

He made good time for about five hours and then heard a sudden clicking from the instrument panel on the motorcycle. He looked down and saw that one of the dials was lit—the geiger counter—and was registering high rads, moving up into the danger zone. Stone came to a rise in the road as it moved through low, rolling curves in the foothills of the mountain range. He stepped the Harley, sat back in the seat, and whistled. For about six or seven miles ahead was a crater, a huge, perfectly oval crater, so big that it seemed he must be dreaming. The crest of the volcano-like dome must have been nearly half a mile high and a good two miles wide.

The atomic mountain was clearly impassable, and if it was registering dangerous radiation readings of a thousand millirems at this distance, he didn't want to think what it was like at ground zero. He knew it must have been a ten megatoner, maybe even a twenty that had hit there. Though he couldn't imagine what there could have been out here in the middle of nowhere for the Russians to have been hunting. Unless, of course, it had just plain missed its target by hundreds of miles. The crater looked more like something that should have been on the moon, than here in his backyard, ripping up the flesh of the earth into a dead zone for miles around. A wound that wouldn't heal for a thousand years.

At any rate, he sure as hell wasn't going to be the first explorer to map its interior. Stone pulled off the road and drove down a cattle track that was heading in a vague westerly direction. At first the going was fairly smooth, but after about twenty minutes the cow-cleared countryside gave way to wild vegetation, bushes several feet high, fields of dead wheat as high as his chest, spreading off in blankets of black and brown. Stone just went through it all, the immense Harley smashing right over the dead stalks and the thorn-bushes like barbed wire. The super-gridded, triple-vulcanized tires had thick crisscrossing treads that worked almost like paddle wheels digging into whatever was beneath and pushing the bike forward. The Harley felt unstoppable beneath his body, like a steel steed that could run over anything.

With the insects buzzing and the birds chirping all around him, Stone drove through the sun-drenched afternoon, filled with the wild meadows and forests of the lower Rockies. Drove as the sun swam from the crystal seas of afternoon into the cobalt-blue rivers of evening and then sank into the purple-black pool of night where it disappeared in a sudden puff of burning red. Drove as the moon rose on silver threads into the star-speckled mega-galaxies of night. Stone couldn't stop moving—not with April's face filling his mind, screaming silently within his brain. Not when he couldn't stop remembering what the bastards had done to his mother— before they killed her. And now Stone's sister, the only one of his family, of his blood left, was in the hands of someone far sicker than any of the Guardians of Hell. For the Dwarf took the word *sadism* to a new level of definition. And

Stone knew if he didn't save her, April was going to be the psychotic quadriplegic's next experiment into the pleasures that pain can bring.

The moon was almost dead high, sitting above his shoulder like a white vulture, when Stone heard the first growl come from a large boulder to his right. Excaliber, who had been feigning sleep for hours but who actually had been totally awake, in pain, and holding on to the Harley for dear life, trying not to vomit up his previous night's takings, heard the growl, too, and suddenly shot up on the seat, standing on its hind legs and resting its good paw on Stone's shoulder as if to see—and to warn him at the same time that something was up.

But Stone could see that something was up—all by himself.

The gap between two immense boulders toward which the Harley was heading was suddenly filled with hurtling dark shapes blocking the way. He slowed the bike, edging his finger toward the trigger on the right handlebar. More and more of the large, thick shapes jumped from their ambush places behind rocks and bushes. And before he knew it, Stone and the pit bull were surrounded by nearly twenty timber wolves, ringing the bike in a nearly perfect circle around him, about thirty feet away. Their eyes glowed in the dark like blazing fireflies, dark red with streaks of golden fire. Eyes everywhere, all staring at him, all hungering to rip his flesh from his bones in long, bloody strips and gulp them down like the finest of prime cuts. Stone moved slowly and spat through his teeth for the pit bull to shut up and stop its low growling, which came out of the opened jaws like a rumbling threshing machine. Stone hadn't stopped moving, though the bike was slowed to just a few miles an hour and beginning to wobble slightly back and forth. If he moved suddenly, they might all jump. If he didn't—He made the decision.

"Down," he screamed to the bull terrier as he squeezed hard on the trigger of the 50-caliber machine gun mounted on the front fender of the Harley. A stream of finger-sized slugs poured out of the front of the bike and toward the four timber wolves who stood blocking the way, big silver-haired things with jaws far apart and incisors as long as kitchen knives. The moment he pulled the trigger, Stone turned the accelerator on the handlebar, and the bike shot forward toward the space created by the four bleeding carcasses that lay twitching dead ahead. But he had gone but a yard or two when he felt the dog suddenly jump from the back of the bike and run—or hobble, really—on three working legs toward the fray, as if to say, "Okay, you twenty mothers, let's get at it."

"Fucking idiot," Stone screamed as he slammed on the brakes of the Harley so hard that the wheels dug deep trenches in the black dirt below. He turned in the seat, ripping out the 12-gauge BPS from its quick-draw saddlebag attached to the left side of the Electraglide and pulled it to chest level, searching for the damned dog. Suddenly he heard sharp growls and then the snapping jaws and wild hisses of several animals. The moon peered from behind a cumulus cloud, and the scene was illuminated with the brilliance of a flare going off.

"Christ almighty." Stone groaned, for the pit bull seemed

to be in the middle of three black-and-silver balls of fur, the entire mass of howling, snapping animals moving at a blur in a tight circle on the ground, already soaked with blood. Suddenly the blur stopped, and Stone saw a huge old wolf fall to the ground, its neck torn open as another younger male pulled back limping, one of its paws gone, a bloody stump scraping along the ground. Only the third was left, and it stood feet away from Excaliber, trying to stare him down. But the pit bull would have none of that. It pointed forward, its nose aiming straight at the timber wolf's throat, its legs bent as if it were posing for a statue of itself in the Royal British Museum. Two down, only eighteen to go. Its wild brown eyes glowed like amber fires in the night.

Two of the wolves nearest the cycle suddenly launched themselves forward, as if starting the hundred-yard dash with Stone's face as the prize. He waited until they were within fifteen feet and then fired once at the foot of air between them. The shot spread out, catching each carnivore dead on in the guts. They spun out in almost symmetrical circles, their intestines and the rotting remains of an elk they had eaten three days before spewing out over the snow. Stone pumped the shell free and spun back to the dog.

"Get your fucking macho ass over here right now! We're leaving!" He whistled twice, as hard as he could, an ear-splitting sound between his teeth that made even the wolves look startled, the hair rising up on their backs for a second as they hunched down low, defensive, uncertain. Excaliber finally seemed to understand that his master didn't want them to stay and fight it out with a wolf pack that looked ready to go down to the last animal. The pit bull snarled once more at the animal that stood crouched down low a yard away from it, trying to get up the courage to leap at the strange animal that had already killed the leader of the pack and one of the elders.

In a flash, like a jackrabbit disappearing behind a bush, the pit bull turned and started toward the bike before the mountain wolves even realized what was happening. Stone threw the Harley into gear and started forward slowly, both feet dragging along the ice-splattered, black ground.

"Come on, come on," he screamed as the terrier rushed forward, nearly falling once or twice, as it still had no use of its wounded leg. The wolves closed in from every side, like a Red Sea of claws and fangs, and Stone released the clutch, shooting ahead to avoid a leaping shape that flew just past his head. Two of the wolves—young, fast ones— were almost on Excaliber, who was still about ten feet from the back of the bike. There wouldn't be time, there wouldn't be fucking time, Stone's mind screamed as he saw the wolves coming. But suddenly the pit bull, in mid-stride, seemed to set down on its powerful back legs in accordionlike fashion and thrust itself up into the air. The ninety-pound container of muscle, as close to steel as animal flesh has ever come, flew like a bird straight through the air and landed with a plop on the backseat, just as the Harley shot forward.

Two more of the timber carnivores launched themselves like rockets from Cape Canaveral, wild-eyed and foaming at the jaws as they tried to get hold of Stone or his murderous little companion. Both human and canine pulled down and forward on the motorcycle, both of them trying to make themselves as streamlined as possible. The wolves hurtled by, misjudging their angle, one of the animal's claws digging into Stone's leather jacket, a new one he had taken from the shelter supply room. Wasn't new anymore, not with wolf hairs and his own blood mixing into the jagged tears of black leather. Fashion in the nineties—it was so hard to keep up with.

The Harley rumbled forward like a battle tank, right through the charging wolves. The front of the bike had been altered and angled with steel sidebars, forming a sort of phalanx of metal. The iron bars slammed through the attack squad like a locomotive through a bunch of cars on the tracks ahead of it and sent them flying, paws and heads hanging at oddly broken angles.

"Go, go," Stone heard himself madly screaming to the bike as he leaned forward, his face touching the bars, accelerating at every second. They were all right on their flanks, he could see as they shot through the gap between the boulders, but a quick glance in the 180-degree rearview mirror showed him that there were a bunch of the slobbering bastards who weren't going to give up and were charging after the Harley, only up to about thirty, with everything they had.

Three pairs of wolf jaws approached the rear of the Electraglide as their meat-grinding mouths snapped open and shut, trying to snag one of Excaliber's legs. The bull terrier turned just as the closest of the timber wolves jumped into the air, as if trying for the world hurdle record. But the pit bull had already set itself, and as the wolf came in, Excaliber whipped his head around from the side and caught the front jaws of the thing between its own bear-trap rows of steel teeth. The pit bull's mouth snapped shut on the wolf, and there was a loud crunching sound as the carnivore's jawbone cracked and shattered. The pit bull swung its head sharply from side to side, three times in each direction, breaking everything a little more, and then spat the load of bloody fur out. The red package of dead meat fell like a rock to the snow behind the now rapidly moving bike and came to a complete and instant stop, thick streams of red pulsing out from beneath its shattered face.

The remainder of the timber wolves had had enough. They stopped hard in their tracks and stared after the Harley, howling with frustration and rage, throwing their red-eyed faces back and screaming out animal dissatisfaction at the moon and the stars.

They nosed around their dead comrades, curious, not really understanding the concept of death, but knowing something was different. That their fellow hunters would not rise again and that a new hierarchy would have to be determined in the pack. They reformed and loped off in the opposite direction of the battle, searching for less well-armed food.

CHAPTER
Six

"THAT WAS really great, dog," Stone shouted around to the pit bull as they drove fast through the cold night air. The land was fairly level again, with just low shrubs, and Stone didn't want to go too slow, in case those back there had cousins in other parts of the county.

"I suppose you thought that was clever, jumping into battle with two dozen thousand-pound throwbacks to the Pleistocene Era. Especially with only three legs. It's mister-tough-dog tonight. New annals of I-don't-give-a-shit Clint Eastwood showdowns of the pit bull terrier breed." The dog barked happily, sure that Stone was thanking it for its help in the battle and again stood up, wrapping its forward paw around his neck and leaning forward so its face was almost alongside his.

"God, god, dog," Stone said with a groan, "you need some heavy-duty conceptual rearrangement about this whole fighting idea here. The main rule is to stay alive. Alive, you hear me? Facing down fifteen tons of hungry mountain wolf is not my idea of staying alive."

The pit bull flicked out a long raspy tongue and licked Stone along the side of the face, getting everything from forehead to chin wet with thick dog taste and smell. Stone shut up and kept going into the endless night with April's face embroidered in dark, bloody stitching across every storm cloud, every curtain of mist that floated through the mountain peaks. They had gone perhaps another hour or so when he couldn't believe his eyes. Lights—and a building of some kind ahead. Four roads including the worn one-laner he had been riding met right in front of the place. As he approached, the engine sinking to a soft putt, Stone read the wooden sign that swung back and forth in front of the old three-story building, lit by an oil lamp set in the shingled wall.

MOM'S INN
WELCOME 24 HOURS A DAY
LEEVE GUNS AT DOOR

An inn. Stone breathed out a deep, ragged sigh. Part of him wanted to just keep going on, but he knew he had to be rational. He'd be no good to April dead, or so tired and run-down that he couldn't function. He pulled the bike over to the front of the place, and a young boy ran from out of the darkness of a stable off to the side.

"Take your bike, mister?" the boy asked, coming up from the shadows until he was on Stone out of nowhere. Stone jerked, almost reaching for one of his guns. Then stopped. He was getting paranoid, crazy. He had to stop.

"Sure, you can take it, but I don't think you could move it. The damned thing's pretty heavy," Stone said as he dismounted and stretched and kicked out his tight, cramped legs. The kid whistled between his teeth, and five more boys ranging in age from about five to seventeen came rushing out of the darkness and up to the bike. Excaliber continued sitting, looking at Stone as if he didn't really want to do a lot of moving around.

"We can take the dog, too, mister—if'n he don't bite," the apparent leader of the group of parking attendants said. "Got nice places for 'em in the back. Get their own stall, with hay to lie in and a fresh trough of water. He'll like it."

"Only thing is he don't get along with other dogs," Stone said, looking down sternly at the errant terrier. "In fact, he doesn't get along with just about everything, I'm afraid."

"Ain't no other dogs here tonight," the boy answered. "Just be him at one end and a couple of mules and horses at the other. Feed him too—all for two bits."

If the battling canine wanted to duke it out with some mules, then let him, Stone decided suddenly, and handed the boy six dollars. "One for each of you, now. But that means you take extra-special care of my bike and my dog, okay?"

"Sure, sure, mister," they yelled out in unison, stepping greedily forward for their prizes. Stone pointed at the dog, commanding it with all the authority he could muster.

"Stay, you hear me! Stay on seat! Go with boys and stay! Eat! Eat more!" The animal looked at him as if he were insane, but had decided for its own reasons to stay and so rested its head back down on its front paws as if waiting to be wheeled off.

"Feed him whatever he wants," Stone said, handing the head barn boy another bill. "Feed him until he drops, until he explodes. Maybe that will keep him sedated." With that he turned and headed up the creaking stairs to the ramshackle, but comfortable-looking, inn. Once through the doors, the smell of rich, thick stew instantly filled his nostrils, then the scent of cigar smoke and the sounds of men talking off in a far room.

"Yes, hello, welcome to Mom's Inn," a pleasant female voice suddenly said to his right. Stone turned, again startled, and looked into the face of an elderly, apple-cheeked woman. "I'm Mom," she said, looking at him from behind a wooden counter. She had a nice face, the kind you felt you could trust instantly, the kind of face your aunt or grandmother might have. And next to her, arms folded across his barrel-sized chest, stood a man a good seven feet tall, not holding any weapon but just showing his crossed arms with muscles thick enough, it appeared, to rip up oak trees by the roots.

"Will you be eating, gambling, staying the night?" Mom asked.

"Some food and a bed is all I need." Stone smiled back wearily. "I don't really know there were places like this that existed anymore."

"I don't know if others do, but this one does, don't it?" She laughed, and Stone couldn't help but smile along with her. "Now, if you'll just give your weapons to Mr. Johnson here." She pointed to her immense assistant, who tried to smile back but only managed to reveal a set of gnashed-down stumps of teeth, which looked just as good hidden away behind closed lips. "'Cause we're glad to have guests, and I'm sure you'll find our services are first-class," Mom went on, "but we only allow gentlemen and ladies of breeding and manners—not some of the crud and animal slime that drifts, from time to time, into our fine establishment. You understand." She looked sweetly at Stone, hoping he'd just politely hand them over, hoping that Mr. Johnson wouldn't have to squash the nice-looking young man with a sledgehammer fist, as he had to do to so many others.

"Sure, be glad to turn in my firepower for the duration," Stone said, undoing the holster of his Uzi and handing it to the giant who fingered the weapon curiously and then snorted, obviously not understanding a hell of a lot about the mechanics of an automatic pistol or much of anything, for that matter. He placed it inside a safe that stood on the floor behind the counter.

"They'll be safe there, of course?" Stone asked as he took off the mini-cannon of a .44 and handed that also into Mr. Johnson's baseball mitt of a hand.

"It's opened only when we put weapons or gold in, I assure you," the woman went on. "Every one is the same in here—that is, without their firepower." Once his pistols were sealed away, Mom took Stone into the dining room and had a bowlfull of rich, steaming goat stew brought in to him. Stone ate it and then another, and the waitress gave him a key with a number on it—his room on the second floor. He started off to bed, looking at a big grandfather clock in the hall, it was nearly two-thirty, but his attention was drawn by hard laughter and the sounds of cards slapping down on a table. He followed the sounds to their source, going through a dark living room with its sofa and couches all draped with plastic coverings, and into another room, a den where ten men were playing cards beneath the light of two hanging oil lamps.

A few of the faces peered up as Stone walked into the room, but their attention instantly reverted back to the round, green, felt-topped card table. One of the men had just won a large pot from the last hand and was sweeping it toward him. The winnings contained dollar bills, silver coins, a gold timepiece, and what looked like some sterling silver spoons and forks. The winner didn't seem to mind that his treasure was of such a hybrid nature and pulled it toward his chest and into the handkerchief he whipped from his breast pocket. The man wore a high top hat, black and shiny, a bow tie, and a precisely pressed double-breasted jacket. With his little straight billygoat goatee and glass eyepiece, which he held squinting between his right eye muscles, the man looked like something Mark Twain might have written about, a Southern gentleman of most eccentric manner.

"Looks like I just can't help but win," the fellow said with the hint of a Southern drawl, though his accent was hard to pin down.

"Can't help but cheat, you mean," a sour-faced player spat out from across the table.

"Now, how could I be cheating, my good fellow," the winner said, "when they're not my cards and I'm not even dealing?"

"Don't know how, just know I want a chance to win my money back—and this time I keep an eye on you." The man positively sneered as he spoke, and Stone saw under the shadows of the man's wide-brimmed hat and looked away quickly, for the face was ugly, filled with acne scars and boils like little volcanoes, some of them oozing as he sat there, sending streams of pink and white down his cheeks. Stone had seen that kind of wound before—radiation poisoning. When it was that bad, you usually didn't live too long. And you had nothing to lose.

"But of course," the goateed man replied with a little flourish of a bow, "I had no intention of leaving yet. Why, it's early." He laughed. "And I'm having so much fun." He threw out a gold watch as the ante to the next hand, dealer's choice.

"Mind if I sit in?" Stone asked, starting to sit down in an empty wooden chair before anyone even answered.

"Sure," said the dealer, an old man with darting, narrow eyes and a long silver beard that came down nearly to his stomach. "It's dealer's choice—only I'm always the dealer, seeing as how it's my place and my cards."

"Sounds fine to me," Stone said, leaning forward, resting both elbows on the table. The waitress appeared out of nowhere and handed him a beer, the tavern's own home-brewed special, with a little hand-drawn picture of Mom on the side. Stone took a swig. The stuff was delicious.

"So, now we're playing five-card draw—'cause that's my favorite game. Anyone mind?" The old dealer sucked hard on his nearly toothless mouth and looked around challengingly like a prune ready to pick a fight. But none of the players present gave a damn. They were happy to have any action at all here in the vast wastelands. The dealer dealt out the cards, and the men took them, holding them up in cupped hands, guarding the faces from prying eyes. They bet, took their second set of cards, and the betting action got hot and furious as both Stone, the goateed fellow, and the man who had accused him of cheating all began raising and raising one another until the center of the table was filled with cash. Stone was betting shimmering, mint silver dollars, thousands of which his father had had stocked in the shelter.

"Call you," the dour-faced fellow said hoarsely, and Stone noticed for the first time that he had a long purplish scar nearly an inch thick that ran clear around his neck, as if someone had sewn his whole damned head on at some point. The man threw down his hand, a full house, three fives and a pair of jacks. Stone threw down his straight, ace low, with a grin, and the man blanched. But before Stone could even think of taking the winnings that sat glowing like a fire of wealth in the center of the table, the goateed man silently lay his hand out across the green felt, spreading the cards without a whisper. He was obviously an expert with cards, perhaps even a hustler.

"I'm sorry to disappoint both of you fine gentlemen," he said, his eyes staring down at the cards, "because I've got a straight flush, queen high." The acne-pitted face across from him tightened up even smaller and meaner than it had already been.

"No way, cheat—nobody gets a hand like that. I ain't never seen a straight flush in all my days of playing!"

"Well, aren't you in luck, then," the goateed man said with a thin smile. "'Cause now you can say you have."

Then everything seemed to move in slow motion. The scar-faced man jumped up, sending his chair flying off behind him. From each side of his buckskin jacket he ripped small pistols and swung them around, searching for blood. But as he moved, both Stone's and the goateed man's own hands whipped like snakes into their clothing and came out with weapons—Stone with a small .38 snub-nosed mini, and the goateed winner with a nickel-plated derringer from beneath his top hat, which shimmered a luminous blue as the oil lamp's rays streaked down on it. The two men opened fire simultaneously. Two holes appeared just inches apart on the scarred man's forehead. His head flew up, making the hat fly off, and they saw just how badly mutilated he had been. Not that it mattered anymore. His arms flew out like chicken wings, and the pistols flew from his hands as if he were throwing the shotput. The scarred face seemed to get the strangest expression, as if he were looking into God's face or something.

"Gee," he said very softly, with just the hint of a smile on his puffed, pus-dripping lips. "Gee," he whispered again, almost inaudibly. Then his eyes rolled up so only white like an egg filled the socket, and he slammed down, crashing face first right into the table, splattering a flood of red over the clean green felt. The man who had been sitting next to him was apparently his pal as well, for he, too, reached for some kind of long, pipelike pistol. But he had barely gotten it free of his long sheepskin coat when a voice boomed through the powder-stenched air.

"Hold it, goddammit, or everyone gets it!" It was Mom, holding a huge blunderbuss of a World War I rifle that looked as if it could take out the whole table and then the wall behind it. "Put your guns down. Now! Now!" If Mom had looked sweet before, she looked positively murderous now, her face beet red, the veins in her neck standing out like cords of pulsing rope.

Stone and the goateed man slowly moved their hands forward to lay the pistols down on the wet tabletop. But the dead man's poker pal made a move with his pistol, trying to sight the goatee in his barrel. The huge rifle roared from across the room, and the man was suddenly lifted bodily and thrown over the table a good eight feet, where he slammed into the wall breaking a picture of an old man standing in front of a mule and slid to the floor, his chest completely torn apart, so that the stuffing of his bloody lungs poured out.

"Told him not to move," Mom shouted, starting forward. She could see that Stone and the goatee were not going to be a threat and put the gun down, slamming the butt next to her foot. The seven-foot Mr. Johnson came in on the run, but she calmed him down and ordered him to remove the corpses to the dump.

"All right," she said as she collected their extra weapons. "I told you guys—no guns. What is it with everyone? Just gotta have one or else you feel naked."

"Madam," the goateed man said, "if I hadn't had this little derringer that me daddy gave me when I was just a lad, you'd be telling your thyroid mutant over there to be carrying *me* out, instead of our radioactive friend on the table there."

"Well, I don't care. Both of you is no longer welcome. You'll be leaving in the morning. I'd throw both of you out tonight, exceptin' there's a storm brewing and you'd die out there. But first thing it clears tomorrow—out!" She led both of them back down the hall and toward their rooms like a schoolmarm, only this one was carrying a rifle that could take out an elephant, and she locked them in their rooms like errant children.

"I'll unlock you in the morning. Don't try anything, 'cause I'm going to be sitting out here with this big bertha here. And I'll blast your goddamned cocks off if you so much as step out to take a piss." Thus spake Mom, and somehow they both believed her.

CHAPTER
Seven

MOM AWOKE them both around noon when the funereal sky lightened slightly and the snows stopped. She fed them each a hot-soup lunch and then handed them some quail sandwiches to take on the road. As hard as she tried, the old woman obviously had a soft spot in her heart, a place for the lonely traveler.

"Now, I know those other fellows was up to no good. And that basically"—she gave them both a quick once-over—"you fellas are all right, give or take a few basic flaws that all men have. So I just thought I'd let you know, 'cause I knowed it was hanging heavy on your hearts—you all are welcome to come back." Mom smiled as she walked them both to the front door. "But next time we're going to strip you naked—look everywhere and make sure there ain't no damned guns." She handed them their weapons as soon as they were actually off the premises, laughed, and slammed the door behind her to keep out the windblown snow, which careened through the slivers of noonday sun, piercing the cloud cover here and there, hinting of more bad weather to come.

"Thanks," the goateed man said as he walked alongside Stone, carrying a rope-tied wreck of a suitcase swinging alongside him.

"For what?" Stone asked, looking over as they both headed toward the garage where their vehicles were stored about fifty yards from the main house.

"For last night. You saved my ass. Name's Dr. Abraham Reagan Kennedy. Call me 'Snake doctor' for short. Pleased to meet you." He held out a hand.

"Mine's Stone, Martin Stone, but to tell you the truth, I was looking out for my own ass. I thought that son-of-a-bitch was trying to take a shot at me. But I'm pleased to meet you, Dr. Kennedy." He shook hands with the man. "Uh, tell me," Stone said, looking over with a nervous grin, "were you cheating?"

"Of course I was cheating. Everyone at that table was cheating. Except you. It was just a question of who was better at cheating than everyone else. And I was the best— by far. Our recently deceased friend was quite bad at it. Why, at one point several cards slipped from his sleeve and fell to the floor. But I knew you were honest. And that you probably didn't even know what was going on."

"Don't make me feel like an idiot from the boondocks or anything." Stone laughed.

"Where are you heading?" the top-hatted cardsharp asked as they opened the garage door and looked in, trying to find the boys who handled the operation.

"Utah—Vernal, Utah," Stone said. "I'm going to this resort there called ... The Final Resort, run by—"

"Yeah, I know who it's run by," Kennedy said, his face growing cold. "I don't think you really want to be visiting a place like that, my innocent friend. That 'resort' is a den of cutthroats, psychotics, perverts, blood sadists, and worse."

"That's the kind of place I always go on vacation," Stone answered.

"Hey, you! Kid!" Kennedy yelled out as he caught sight of a shadow at the far end of the huge garage that had once been a horse barn.

"Yeah, mister," the teenager said, running quickly over in bare feet to the two men.

"Time to leave—I'm taking my truck. You filled her with water, cleaned her off like I told you?"

"Sure did, mister." The kid smiled, revealing huge gaps of a number of missing teeth in the front of his mouth. Kennedy handed him two quarters.

"How come you're not wearing shoes," Stone asked, looking down at the boy's frigid, nearly blue feet.

"Mom won't let us—says it toughens up the feet and soles when you go around with nothing on 'em." The youth smiled again.

"Nice lady, Mom." Dr. Kennedy grinned at Stone as he started forward to his truck, a huge, lumbering-looking vehicle that was parked off to their right, facing the wooden wall. Stone whistled as he saw what had once been a moving truck with high roof and wide, thick walls. The thing looked like a mobile house—with tin chimney on top and thick, heavily treaded tires that looked like they came from a military vehicle.

"Home, sweet home," Kennedy said as he opened the back doors of the vehicle, swinging them wide apart. "Want to take a look inside?" Without even waiting for a reply, Dr. Kennedy pulled down some folding wooden steps and walked up and inside the truck. He flicked a switch just inside the door, and the truck lit up like a showroom. Stone and the barefoot kid who stood behind him craning his neck to see in both gasped, for the innards of the ancient truck were filled with colors and shapes of every size and description. It was like a traveling bazaar, a mobile flea market. Everything one could imagine seemed to adorn the walls or hang from the ceiling.

There were foxtails, bicycle frames, dishes, books, hooks, fishing poles, rifles, tennis rackets, snakeskins, foxskins, bearskins. There were sets of eating ware, pots and pans, sheets, dresses, socks, shaving equipment, and ammunitions. There was a grinding wheel, a barber's chair, a mirror, a stethoscope, a fire ax and extinguisher, and two sinks. There were irons, hammers, crowbars, wheels of every size, toothbrushes, dolls and stuffed animals, masks, feathers, chains, coils of ropes, chairs. There was more stuff packed into one place than Martin Stone had ever seen in his life. It seemed as if you could look forever and still not find the end of what was contained within. For everywhere that his eyes rested were just layers and layers of objects—jewels, mooseheads . . .

"It's more of a secondhand store than a home," Stone grunted as he stood dazed just inside the doorway.

"'Tis home to me," Kennedy said with a satisfied smile as he dropped the suitcase he was carrying containing his winnings from the previous night's poker game, and reached for a bottle sitting on top of a nearby wicker table with golf clubs and a pile of horseshoes lying on top of it and a stack of what looked like umbrellas beneath it.

"Care for a swig—it's Dr. Kennedy's Certified Snake Oil and Medicinal Alcoholic Preparation. Good for anything that ails you." He leaned his head back, put one hand around his goatee, gathering it together so that it wouldn't get wet, and took a huge draw from the bottle. He gulped, seemed to turn lobster red for a few seconds, and then let out a thunderous explosion of sound, somewhere between a sneeze and a scream.

"Damn, that's a strong batch!" He laughed, his eyes watering up. "Puts hair on your balls—I'll tell you that, son." Stone couldn't resist and took the proffered bottle, closed his eyes, leaned back, and gulped down a decent amount of the super elixir. It was like a river of fire had entered his gullet, and it was all he could do not to spit the stuff up again. He made strange sounds between his lips, blowing out as if trying to put out a fire, and his eyes likewise watered up so tears dripped out from the sides.

"You . . . drink this stuff all the time?" Stone asked when he could finally speak again, waving his hand across his mouth to try to cool off the flames inside.

"All the time," Dr. Kennedy deadpanned, taking another swig. "Yes, this is me elixir laboratory, me home, me storage, me magic factory, me every bloody thing," the man said, sweeping his hands proudly around the inside of the truck, talking with what Stone swore was a bad Irish accent now, when before it had been a bad Southern one.

"What exactly do you do?" Stone asked as he stood just inside the truck, afraid to move forward for fear of getting lost inside and never seeing the light of day again.

"I'm a traveling salesman, a magician, a card-playing, pistol-packing hypnotist huckster, Stone. I'll heal your wife, give you a love potion, fix your rheumatism, mend your cow. I'll make your crops grow, write you a will, cook you a feast, give you pills for your diarrhea. I'll cure all your ills—from influenza to typhoid fever, from canker sore to cancer—all with my Dr. Kennedy's Certified Snake Oil here." Now he seemed to be speaking with a bad New England accent, as if he really were his namesake, President Kennedy himself, at his finest hour.

He paused as the speech had been spoken in one long breath, sucked in air, and then started out again. "Anything that you need, I have—somewhere in my truck, Mr. Stone. I am loved by the people of this poor wreck of a nation because I bring them what they want most—new things, satins and silks, shiny pots and pans. It is not just appliances I sell, Mr. Stone—but hope itself. I travel the highways and byways of America, bringing wares and services to those that need them—but to whom no one comes—though they wait, eyes wide, by the road, for something, some connection with the world. I am the original, all-purpose, Yankee Doodle Dandy, spreading my wares, a Johnny Appleseed of odds and ends—and how may I be of service?" He finished the Shakespearean soliloquy with a bow, taking off his top hat and sweeping it across his waist.

"Good God," Stone mumbled through his teeth. "I—I—"

"Don't say a word, lad. I know I often leave them speechless." He moved forward, and Stone jumped back down to the dirt of the old barn, now patched with shining little half-dried puddles of oil. Dr. Kennedy followed and relocked the door. He walked with Stone as the garage worker led them to the motorcycle parked about eighty feet away near a window that let in a stream of pulsing silver light as the clouds above danced in anticipation of their imminent release.

"Fed yur dog like you said, mister," the nearly toothless boy said. "Just kept eating and eating. What's wrong with that animal? I ain't never seen no dog go at it like that. What d'ya starve him or something?" Stone resisted squashing the lad beneath his boot and shook his head as he saw Excaliber lying on his side again, eyes tightly shut, paws and bottom pulled up in a fetal position as if he were searching for just the right angle that would relieve the pain. A bowl the size of a ten-gallon bucket sat in front of him with but a few crumbs of mashed biscuit and horsemeat left on the bottom.

"It was full when we gave it to him, I swear," the kid said, folding his arms and looking down severely at the pit bull. "We was going to feed half of it to some other dogs out in the yard but never got the chance." Stone pulled out another silver dollar, shining like ice as the sun stabbed through the dusty window, igniting the barn with light.

"Here. He's been a little upset lately—since he hurt his paw. Insecure, you know. The food makes him feel better."

"Just needs some Certified Snake Oil," Dr. Kennedy said, pulling out a silver flask from his white jacket's inner pocket. "Here, boy, here." He got down on one knee and petted the dog softly. Excaliber rolled over and stared up through one half-opened eye, examining the strange being before it. "Fix tummy, fix tummy good," the man spoke in singsong words. He held the flask down, and Excaliber opened his jaws, taking some in. The huckster instantly pulled back as Excaliber jumped to his legs and seemed to vibrate and begin bucking around like a bronco, spinning and leaping into the air. He did this dance for about six seconds, then slowed, just turning a few quick circles as if chasing his tail, and then came to a complete stop. The dog looked up at Stone, shook its head as if to get the cobwebs out, and then barked, wagging its tail. It walked the few feet to Dr. Kennedy and licked his hands, looking imploringly up for more.

"Friend for life." Stone smirked with disgust. "That dog is getting to be a regular hedonist—feasts every night of at least ten courses or ten pounds, whichever comes first, and now fine liqueurs. You're going to instill expensive tastes in what is basically a poverty-stricken animal."

"Listen—I have a proposal, Stone," the snake-oil salesman said, patting Excaliber behind the ears, the spot he loved most. "Believe it or not, I'm heading to the Retreat too. I put on a Christmas show there each year. I can get into the place—you couldn't even do it on your own—believe me. The security is heavy-duty. Come with me—in the truck. I know the way. Could use the company. It would add maybe one extra day to your trip. Maybe not even that much, since I know a shortcut. What d'ya say? I could use the company. Man get's lonely traveling through the wastelands by himself year after year. Be nice just to have another voice to talk to."

Stone looked the goateed man straight in the eyes. His skin was old, weathered, sun-baked leather with lines and little wrinkles spreading off like ripples throughout the face. But the eyes were young and sparkled with mischief like a child's, as if they found it all, even the terrors of the post-nuke world, a place one could find humor in, even laugh at. Whatever the man's "unusual" qualities, Stone knew he could trust him with his life.

"Sounds okay," he answered, looking down at Excaliber, whom the doc had eating out of the palm of his hand. He'd never seen the dog respond quite like that to anyone, even himself. And in spite of himself, Stone almost felt a twinge of jealousy. "But what the hell will I do with my bike? Thing's a monster."

"We'll just load her up into the truck," Dr. Kennedy said, looking at the Harley. "Had bigger things than that in there— had a whole damned car in there once—took it nearly a thousand miles where I sold it to a man for his two daughters—and pretty ones they was, at that." Stone couldn't tell half the time if Kennedy was playing with him or not. With that amused look in his eye he always seemed to be engaging in some sort of game with whomever he was talking to.

Stone wheeled the bike over to the truck where the doctor of philosophy, science, and the occult, with fifteen degrees hanging on the inside of the truck's walls, had already pulled a long lever at the back. A hidden metal platform wheezed out from beneath the floor of the truck and then slowly lowered itself down until it clanked heavily on the hard barn dirt.

"You sure this thing can take it?" Stone asked nervously, since the bike was as heavy as a rhino.

"Of course, of course." Kennedy waved him on impatiently, and Stone rolled the Electraglide onto the steel ramp and stood beside the bike holding it. The doctor pushed the lever forward again, and the steel platform started up. It moved, but as slow as a turtle, everything grinding together as if the pully system might explode at any moment. The entire truck shook from side to side, as the back part of the frame sank a good four inches down on the old suspension. But the platform kept rising, chugging, grinding away as if it were about to have a heart attack. It took nearly three minutes for the machine to pull the Harley up, but at last, to Stone's amazement, he was level with the truck floor and wheeled the bike in to a space where the doc had just sort of kicked a few tables out of the way.

They locked up in back and got into the driver's seat, the teenage garage attendant's jaw hanging open, as it had been for about fifteen minutes. He stared at Kennedy as if he were from another planet, with awe and superstitious fear. The man did have magic. Real magic. Of that the lad was sure. Stone got in from the right driver's seat and the pit bull jumped up too, quickly finding a comfortable spot between the two men's legs, its body wrapped like a snake around the casing of the gearshift.

The boy opened the huge barn doors, and the truck started forward, coughing and jerking around as if it were about to have a seizure. They drove out, taking the widest of the four roads that intersected in front of Mom's Inn and headed west.

"About your accents," Stone said as he rested an elbow on the glassless window frame and breathed in the cold winter air. "They keep changing. What are you? Southern? Irish? New Englander?"

"I'm whatever you want me to be," the snake-oil salesman said with a quick laugh. "Whatever you hear."

CHAPTER
Eight

THE WINTER sky overhead looked mean. The clouds formed claws and teeth with which they would mock-dive at the earth, pulling up at the last moment. But something was brewing up there. The wind rushed in through the open windows of the truck, and Stone at last pulled the turtleneck of his sweater all the way up so it covered the right side of his face and neck.

"Don't believe in windows?" he asked Dr. Kennedy.

"Luxuries," the huckster spat back. "Makes you soft. No, whatever you do to yourself, make it hard, harder than that which you encounter in the world. That way you'll always be prepared. Cold air's good for you. Finest thing in the world. Next to snake oil, a lungful of nearly frozen mountain oxygen will cure you of all lung diseases, including worm infestation." He leaned his head out of the window, sucking in a mouthful of the burning Rocky Mountain air, and slammed a few times on the horn as he pulled back in. "Shit, that feels good." The dog, preferring in its animal wisdom to seek warmth rather than cold, lay curled up like a ball between the two men's legs, soaking up every bit of body heat it could.

"Tell me," Stone asked curiously, turning back to the snake-oil salesman, who squinted hard at the road ahead, wiping the inside of the filth-splattered windshield with the sleeve of his jacket. "How did you ever become the great healer of the masses that you are now?"

"Ah me, lad," Dr. Kennedy said, this time in heavy brogue. "The story is too long to tell the full tale of. Besides, it would make your young ears burn with horror. The things I've seen and done are not for mortal man to know. But suffice it to say, I was born of a murderous sailor who was hung on me mother's wedding night and a two-hundred-pound whore whose specialty was whipping men with a riding crop. I was raised by the prostitutes and pimps of numerous fine establishments throughout the south and learned at a young age how to—shall we say—fend for myself. I was fortunate enough that one of my mother's clients was a quite well-educated gentleman of Southern aristocracy who saw in me an extremely intelligent, if misguided, youth. He taught me to read and gave me use of his immense library.

"My schooling was the streets and this man's library where I devoured everything with a voracious appetite. All of Shakespeare, Chekov, Voltaire, Stendahl, Proust. Then the English poets. I studied the Greek philosophers, then Kant, Hegel, and Marx. I learned my doctoring skills from anatomy charts, and potion-mixing from chemistry tables. It was all there, Stone, all the knowledge of mankind, just sitting in those pages. And I knew, could see even then, that knowledge was power. And I was going to learn every goddamned thing I could—on every subject—and use it all to aid my survival." The doctor looked quickly out the window, his eyes going up to the twisting skies that grew darker and thicker with every minute.

"Anyway, as I said, to make a long story short, because I'm not even going to get into my years breeding cattle, running guns in Latin America, or my explorations in Tibet, that's what I've done. Used my knowledge. My knowledge of everything—to help people. Before the war—and since—I've spent my life bringing life to the little people who spend their drab existences in the middle of nowhere getting sick and allowing their knives to become dull. Those in need of an elixir, a new pan, or a new idea are my flock."

Whenever Dr. Kennedy got talking, his eyes would glaze over, and he seemed to go into an almost trancelike state—the mystical ecstasies of a snake-oil salesman in the full gallop of his sales pitch. But the man's mouth looked worried as he glanced out the window again and again.

"Sky's looking pretty funny," Stone said, looking out from his side. It wasn't just the thick purple-and-black clouds crashing and melting into one another high above them, nor the cracks of distant lightning and thunder which they began hearing, that was a little disconcerting. It was the greenish color of the sky everywhere around them. A color of vomit, of flesh long dead. A vibrating green with pools of squash yellow mixed in. The whole thing mixed slowly together around them in mile-wide circles like mush turning in a blender. The air pressure in both men's ears suddenly changed dramatically, and their eardrums popped and made clicking sounds as they worked their jaws to relieve the pressure. Excaliber felt it, too, and sat up suddenly, cracking his jaws as far apart as they would go and letting out a little howl of displeasure.

"I've never seen a sky quite like that," Stone said, feeling his heart beating faster from the sheer mood of the heavens.

"I have," Kennedy said with the softest tones Stone had heard him speak in. "Just once, two years ago. Saw one go by far off from a mountain. Didn't get me, but it got other things. It was . . . horrible. Like a mixture of a tornado and a blizzard and a sandstorm—and every goddamned kind of bad weather you can imagine all rolled into one, everything twisting around at a thousand miles an hour."

"Jesus, you think this could be another one?" Stone asked as the pit bull jumped over to his side and put its paws up on the sill with its head half out the window to see what the hell was going on up above. It looked and then turned to Stone with a most concerned expression, not liking the color of the sky at all. It withdrew down to its previous position between their legs, curled up into a fetal ball with its paws over his nose and eyes, so it wouldn't have to see a thing when the end came and thus seceded from reality.

"I think it is one," Dr. Kennedy answered as the truck went over a huge pothole in the road and all its occupants were tossed about a foot in the air and then dropped hard in the exact same spots. As if to agree with the snake oiler's assessment, the sky suddenly rippled with waves of yellow and blue electricity. The curtains of shimmering energy looked like the aurora borealis, only these were dancing through the thunderclouds and they were flying low, very low.

Suddenly loud pings came against the front windshield, and Stone felt sharp slaps against his hand and arm. Hailstones—the size of Ping-Pong balls—were falling everywhere. Within seconds the truck was being pelted with the hard balls of frozen ice. It sounded like a billion fingers clawing above their heads as the stones slammed onto the metal rooftop and echoed through the truck's walls. The sound was deafening, and Excaliber began howling just to add some higher frequencies to the improv jam session.

Kennedy slowed the house-sized truck to a crawl, as he could barely see through the windshield, so inundated was it with the storm of ice. Then the lightning started. The first bolt hit about a hundred yards off but felt like it was next door. A jagged thirty-foot-wide piece of twenty million volts of electricity stabbing into the top of a pine tree and sending fir branches flying in flaming circles through the air. Then they started striking everywhere, bolt after bolt sizzling down from the heavens, spears of blinding white that sent dirt flying and cracked boulders in two like a diamond cutter's fine chisel.

One hit just yards ahead of the truck, then another off to the side, slashing sideways into a thick tree, slicing it in two with a shower of sparks and wrenching roots. The whole world seemed to be afire. Then the sky opened up. It was as if the clouds had been holding their vast loads of subfreezing moisture behind the walls of an immense dam. And now the gates were opened. An icy rain came down on them in solid sheets of impenetrable slush. The truck suddenly seemed to be in the middle of a sea of ice and sleet.

The snake doctor brought the truck to a halt and turned to Stone who was crouching back in the seat, arms flat on his legs, trying not to touch any metal in case, or rather, when, one of the bolts slammed into the truck. It was only a matter of time.

"Listen," Kennedy said. "I know this is probably going to sound insane, but we have to go out there and tie this mother down"—he patted the seat of the truck—"because this storm is going through exactly the same evolution as the last one I saw—and that means it's going to get worse before it gets better." As Stone didn't particularly like sitting in the middle of a shooting gallery of supercharged energy, he nodded.

They both threw open their doors simultaneously and ran to the back of the truck through the driving sleet that filled the air. Kennedy reached underneath the back frame of the huge vehicle and opened a supply box, quickly hauling out what looked like long cables of steel.

"These are heavy-duty construction cables—used to be used to raise and lower a crane. I'll throw them over the top—you catch them on the other side and then attach them to the ground with these bolts. Okay?" Stone nodded, though it was hard to hear through the thundering crashes all around them. The doc handed him an armload of two-foot-long spikes and a twenty-pound sledgehammer. Stone moved carefully around the back of the truck, trying not to slide on the increasingly slippery surface of the iced-over ground. The sleet and rain were coming in fast and at a nearly horizontal angle, so the sharp flakes and crystals of ice felt as if they were actually cutting into his cheeks and nose and eyelids.

Stone threw the whole mess down on the soggy ground and stared up waiting for the cable to come flying over. Within seconds it did, the two-inch-thick cable flailing about like a snake looking for a hole. He caught it and hooked one of the long spikes through the steel eye at the end. With all his weight he plunged the sharp tip of the spike into the hard ground and then began pounding it with the sledge so that it grudgingly slid deeper and deeper into the dark, frozen soil.

They pounded in four such steel cables, cradling the truck from front to back, holding it down tightly, latched to the very earth beneath it.

"Now we get inside where it's all nice and warm, right?" Stone asked hopefully as he walked around to the snake-oil king who was pounding in the last of his pegs.

"No—now we go *under* the truck where maybe, just maybe, we'll live through it all." He reached into the utility box beneath the truck frame and pulled out a long steel rod. Stepping up on a part of the chassis, Dr. Kennedy somehow climbed halfway up the side of the truck and placed the rod into a circular holder on the very top. Then he dropped down fast.

"Under, man, under the truck," he said, motioning with his hands.

"But the dog..." Stone started forward, only to be met by a sudden wall of wind that came down the road toward them with such velocity that it swept both men from their feet and onto their backs. Stone managed to roll over and under the truck where the huge frame and the thick wheels offered some protection.

"Excaliber's still out there," Stone said as he came face-to-face with Kennedy, his face and entire body covered in mud and black sleet.

"Forget it," the jack-of-all-trades yelled through the rising gales of wind just feet away. "If we live, he lives. If we don't, you might need a dog in the afterlife. I'm sure God Almighty could use a nice watchdog," Stone started to roll over and out from beneath the truck. But the ferocity of the wind was so strong, he knew he couldn't go an inch. Things flew by past them, branches, thousands of leaves. Then larger things, birds, lizards, tumbling end over end, their clawed feet punching at the air trying to gain a foothold on something.

Stone heard a sound and looked back under the truck behind them. There was a roar coming, a sound that made even the screaming winds and the punching blasts of lightning crashing into every mountain peak pale by comparison. He thought he saw a funnel of black smoke. But it was moving. Yes, coming this way. Jesus, the size of it, Stone thought in awe, as he realized it was a tornado, a spire of pure death, a mile wide, and it was coming straight at them.

"Huh, these cables. They're pretty strong, huh?" Stone screamed out to Dr. Kennedy as they both pulled into the center of the area protected by the wide body of the truck."

"Goddamned right they're strong," Kennedy screamed back. "It's just a little blow. It'll pass in no time—and then we'll be on our way." Even in the midst of the sleet-filled darkness Stone could see the mad look in Kennedy's eyes. The man seemed to thrive on danger, on going to the very limits.

A bolt of lightning suddenly shot right into the roof of the truck, biting into the pole that had been set up. The current flowed in a stream of glowing electrons through the metal frame and then down into the wheels and the earth. Stone, lying two feet from the raised bottom of the truck, sitting high up on its military wheels, could see and feel the current, could feel the hair on his head and chest rise straight up, reaching toward the supercurrent of electricity. Both men hugged the ground like pieces of paper, not daring to let even one of their whiskers touch a piece of metal.

The roar of the approaching tornado grew to the deafening thunder of a locomotive coming down the tracks at them. Stone arched his head, looked toward the back of the truck again, and saw it. The funnel was just yards away from them, making everything as far as the eye could see just a dark, spinning mass of black wind. Inside it he could see animals, cars, barn doors, all twisting and turning as if in a great washing machine in the sky. And he swore as the super tornado came straight toward the truck that he could hear the screams of the animals trapped within.

Then it was on them. The blackness itself enveloped the truck, and the vehicle shook as if in the hands of a giant, an angry giant. The multiton moving truck shook, straining at the bonds that held it down, like a rabid dog struggling to tear free. Stone sucked in air, but there was none to breathe. It was as if the funnel were sucking in even the air from under the truck. He reached up and grabbed hold of a wide piece of the steel frame of the truck and wrapped his arms and legs around. He'd rather be electrocuted than sucked out into the arms of that dark thing.

He turned his head and saw that Kennedy had done the same. And there they hung, like bats, upside down in near pitch blackness as the wind funnel tore and scratched at the truck with all its strength as if frustrated that it could not tear the thing free—when everything else was cooperating so nicely. The funnel held them in its grasp for what seemed like eternity, shrieking with a howl that threatened to explode their eardrums. And then it began weakening, and suddenly it was gone. Moving on to chew up as much of America as it could before its own twisting forces lost symmetry and it died, turning into biting little breezes that ripped bird's nests from their branches and overturned grave stones. It was truly an ill wind, fighting out to the last of its belligerent airs.

The two men slid out from beneath the battered truck. It had a few big dents in its side from flying debris, but amazingly seemed basically whole. The sky was still dark above them, releasing a slow mist of ice steam that felt almost warm. But ahead, where the storm and the tornado plowed on, the horizon was filled with that same sickly green and yellow. The two of them were covered from head to toe with mud and grime, not a clean inch of flesh or clothing showing. They both couldn't help but laugh as they saw the other and knew that they looked just as ridiculous.

They walked to the front of the truck and pulled open their doors simultaneously. Excaliber, sitting in the middle of the seat, cool as a cucumber and dry as a sheet, stared back at Stone with an amused expression, wondering how his master could have gotten so filthy. The dog yawned as if it had been sleeping through the entire event, which was the last straw for Stone.

"Come here, dog," he commanded sternly, standing on the footrest on the side. "Down, down." He pointed at the mud and ice-filled ground. "We swam in it—now your turn. Any dog of mine must share in all my experiences. Down, down." The pit bull resisted for a while, but as all dogs must do when commanded by their masters, he at last rose, walked to the edge of the seat, and looked down at the thick mud with an expression of utter disgust.

"Down!" Stone said sharply, stabbing with his finger toward the filthy ground. As if jumping from an Olympic diving board, the fighting dog leapt from the seat, a good eight feet through the air, and landed with an immense splash in a deep puddle of the black gunk left behind by the storm. He began jumping up and down in it, leaping around in it, twisting his head from side to side as if frolicking in a summer meadow, playing in the wretched stuff. The mocking face looked back at Stone as if saying, "Come on, join me, it's fun," thus denying him even the slightest pleasure at seeing the hound take its mud bath.

CHAPTER
Nine

THEY DROVE west, following right behind the monstrous post-nuke blow, which they could see miles ahead of them, lighting the way forward with its green warning lights. It left a trail of devastation behind it as if a whole row of A-bombs had gone off. Trees littered the entire region like matchsticks fallen from a kitchen box. And animals, ripped to pieces—foxes, deer, woodchucks, skunks, even a bear or two, all had been sucked up into the tornado's whirling rotors of wind and sliced into garbage.

Anything that had come face-to-face with the black whirlwind had come out on the losing end. Pockets of bloody fur were draped everywhere like ornaments on the fir trees, a reminder of the approaching holiday season.

But at last the storm system had veered sharply south, and though it stayed dark and miserable in the skies ahead where they were headed, it was like a balmy day in Bermuda compared to what they had just been through. Both men were in a good mood, as men are prone to be when they've just had their asses pulled from the great beyond by the grace of God and no one and nothing else. Someone, something wanted them to live—because they should be dead. A funnel like that, passing right over them, being inside the damned thing's churning stomach for a few seconds. It made Stone feel humble, made him start to wonder for the first time if what the Ute Indian had told him after they'd rescued him, that Stone was a "Nadi," one with the gift of death—the gift of giving death—was true. He had been spared today. Perhaps he really did have a destiny, a fate beyond his own survival, beyond even his liberating of April.

They drove for hours, the sun staying behind thick cloud cover but providing enough light to see along the dirt road that snaked up and down and through a series of midsized foothills of the western Rockies. At last they passed a dangling sign that read WELCOME TO UTAH, THE BEEHIVE STATE. Within another hour they came to a settlement—people walking around a town square with horses and wagons hitched up to posts in front of about a dozen little wooden stores. Some of the townspeople who had seen the snake-oil man before, on his last trip around, came running over, wanting first dibs on his treasures.

"You'll all get your chance. Come back tonight at eight o'clock. That's three hours from now. Tonight at eight." They looked somewhat disappointed but backed away and headed into the tiny shops, whose paltry stock of items they had already seen a thousand times before. The truck brought new things, treasures, shining and beautiful things. Things that could make a log hovel become a shining thing of beauty when the right "thing" was put there, be it a portrait of the

Queen of England or a stuffed lynx on a walnut pedestal. Soon the whole town was buzzing with the arrival of the "snake man."

Meanwhile Dr. Kennedy pressed Stone into service, having him first help him pull out a huge, folded tarp from the back of the truck—and then erect it, tying one end to runners along the roof and the other to wooden poles in the ground. Within about twenty minutes the overhang was up, then the two of them carried out tables, chairs, boxes of magic tricks, and crates of items for sale—pots and pans, blankets, clothes, a myriad of shining and unusual little appliances, costume jewelry, a bottle or two of perfume, and a large number of uncategorizable items, some of which even Kennedy himself had no idea what the hell they were.

But somehow—out of a bunch of junk—Dr. Kennedy threw together in just an hour or two what looked like a mini carnival, albeit a somewhat bizarre and mostly stuffed one, with two skeletons hanging side by side, a row of giant ostrich eggs on a round marble table with piles of yellow powder next to them, and a two-headed lizard that ran back and forth inside its glass aquarium searching for flies.

Then he started hauling out all the stuffed and mounted heads from the truck, again pressing Stone into service— moose heads, bear heads, huge stags, their horns towering above their marble eyes, all were pulled out from the innards of the truck, given a quick dusting to free them from spiderwebs and dirt and then mounted on the outer wall of the immense vehicle. By the time they were done, nearly thirty of the animal heads were facing forward, looking out toward the crowds that would soon arrive. Even Stone was impressed. There were no elephants, no dancing girls—but out of the back of a moving secondhand store the doctor was creating a whole fantasy world, a veritable poor man's circus.

At exactly the stroke of eight Dr. Kennedy pulled up the side and front flaps of the tarp, and standing on a crate so he looked about nine feet tall and wearing a long cape with arcane symbols and shapes embroidered in gold stitching all over it, he began banging furiously on a deep brass gong that sent out rolling waves of thunderous sound throughout the small settlement. Out they came in their Sunday finest, clothes with but a few holes, garments with every button. Tonight was the event of the year, and you had to be dead or dying of radiation poisoning to miss it.

"That's it, gather 'round, ladies and gentlemen, there's plenty of room. Plenty of room to see everything. Come on in, that's it. Don't be shy, don't be bashful. Welcome to the Dr. Kennedy Circus of Magic. Guaranteed to be unlike anything you've ever seen before."

"Amen," Stone mumbled under his breath, standing about six feet behind Kennedy.

"Presented tonight by" he held up a bottle of his favorite elixir, of which there were twenty boxes stacked neatly just under the truck. "Certified, all-healing, all-nourishing, no artificial flavors, colors, or additives. I'm talking about the one and only, superlative, indescribable, pain-killing, tumor-flushing, snakebite healing, wonder medicine called Dr. Kennedy's Snake Oil." He held up a bottle, letting the glass shine for a moment from the reflecting rays of the four propane lanterns he had strung up on around the truck and on the outer poles that held up the long red-and-white-striped canvas.

Several hands reached up to see the stuff. "Later, my friends, later. Believe me—you will all have a chance to examine for yourselves the miracle of the ages, but first . . ." He dramatically threw the bottle to Stone, who barely caught it off in the shadows. "Let me demonstrate some of nature's mysteries to you all." There was a dramatic puff of smoke that shot about ten feet in the air, and when it cleared, it appeared that Kennedy had moved to the other side of the enclosure. The crowd gasped, and women moved closer to their husbands, children to their mothers.

"And now life from death, death from life." He paused dramatically and waved a silk scarf over three huge eggs that sat on the table before him. Suddenly the one in the middle cracked open and a full-grown bird emerged. Kennedy took the purple-and-blue-feathered thing on his fingers and then raised it to the sky where it took off, disappearing into the night air. The crowd applauded fiercely.

"Oh, that's nothing. We have just begun, ladies and gentlemen. Just begun." For the next hour Dr. Kennedy had the eighty or so men, women, and children spellbound. He did magic tricks, making chicks and rabbits, coins and cards disappear and reappear. He made smoke seem to rise and take on human form and then evaporate when he blew at it. He cut a snake in two and then reassembled it. He pushed spikes through each cheek as the crowd turned their heads in horror and then lifted two hundred-pound weights from each side of his face. And for his final act he spit fire. Not little puffs of flame but huge sheets that filled the enclosure and pushed the townspeople back as they shielded their faces from the heat.

At last the show was over, and Stone helped him drag away some of the refuse. Dr. Kennedy stood before his podium now and raised his fist to the ceiling and pounded it down on the wood so the whole place echoed with a loud smack. Everyone's eyes in the place popped wide open from the sound, a little jolt of adrenaline running through their veins.

"Ladies and gentlemen, the reason I can do all this—the reason I can pierce my flesh and eat fire—is because of one thing only." He held up a bottle of his all-purpose liquid. "Certified Snake Oil. I make it myself, every blessed bottle of it. Wouldn't have it any other way. I drink a bottle when rising in the morning and a bottle before going to sleep at night. And I'm seventy-five years old. Look at me. I say, look at me!" The doc spread his arms and filled his chest with air, pounding himself on the heart vigorously. Then he jumped up and down fast for about ten seconds.

"Find me a seventy-five-year-old man who can do that and I'll, why, I'll pay you two hundred dollars." He pulled out a wad of bills from his pocket and, licking his fingers, began counting out what appeared to be an immense amount of cash.

"Now, look at this man," Kennedy suddenly yelled out, slamming the money back in his pants. Rolling his eyes, Stone stepped forward into the light and the front of the slightly raised platform Kennedy had put up for performing.

"Now, I found this man lying in the dirt just two weeks ago—a pile of skin and bones. And you know what he was suffering from? Do you know what he was suffering from?" the doctor asked with all the fervor of a baptist priest at a revival meeting.

"What?" someone screamed out, near hysteria.

"He was suffering—I should say, dying from—radiation poisoning." The crowd gasped and shook their heads. Tears came to many eyes, for of all the post-nuke diseases that afflicted humanity—radiation poisoning, numerous cancers, and the subsequent conditions of cellular breakdown it created—this had taken more of their loved ones that anything else.

"Yes, radiation poisoning. His face was the color of rotted pumpkin, and his teeth was falling right out of his mouth like a set of busted dice. Now, I found this man, and because I am a doctor and a humanitarian of the highest order, I stopped and did my best. And it was hopeless, hopeless."

"No, no," voices whispered out from around the enclosure, totally wrapped up in Kennedy's mesmerizing sales pitch.

"But I said, Kennedy, you've got to try to save this man, and I did the only thing I knew—I gave him Certified Snake Oil. And you know what, ladies and gentlemen, do you know what the hell happened? Excuse me for cursing—I get overexcited whenever I think about it. This man, this man you see before you right here, was completely and totally cured. Look at this man."

He ran the few feet separating them over to Stone and turned him around so the crowd could see him. Then just as Stone faced forward again, the caped master of ceremonies reached up and opened his mouth like a horse's.

"Look at them perfect teeth. Even the loose ones that were hanging out by their threads are back in place." He put his fingers over the teeth and pulled hard, until Stone pushed his hand away and looked at the master salesman as if he were mad. Before Stone could utter a word, Dr. Kennedy leaned over and pulled out his shirt so his chest and stomach were showing. Suddenly he drew back his fist and punched Stone hard in the stomach before he even knew what was going on.

"Look at that—incredible! You can see it with your own eyes. This man is as healthy and as strong as a mule." Some of the younger, and older, women in the crowd looked shyly up at Stone's strong, young body as he pulled down his shirt.

"So I ask you, ladies and gentlemen—the question is not would you like to buy any Dr. Kennedy's Certified Snake Oil but how many bottles do you want?" He lifted a crate, motioning to Stone with his eyes to grab another, and placed it on the round table on which he had performed his magic tricks. The crowd broke ranks and rushed toward the stage in a frenzy. Hands held up anything of value they possessed—coins, chickens, jewelry, rings. As each hand came close, the doctor looked quickly at what it contained and then handed the payer one, two, or three bottles of the super-liquid, depending on his assessment.

Ten minutes later it was as if they'd just been through another tornado as the doctor collapsed in a chair and Stone looked down at him, his eyes bloodshot. They were all gone—the crowds—carrying dozens of bottles of the stuff, some of them with their arms full. In a world without the slightest bit of medicine snake oil offered the only hope there was.

"That was good, real good," Stone said with a grimace. "Only I didn't know I was going to be used for demonstration purposes."

"Oh, didn't we go through that? Of course, I'll pay you as my assistant. Here." He threw Stone a little wristwatch computer that was still working, showing time, date...

"Thanks but no thanks," Stone said, throwing the watch back the moment he caught it. "Don't you feel at all guilty about taking all those poor suckers for what little they've got?"

"Listen, friend," Dr. Kennedy said, leaning back and putting his arms behind his head as if he felt not the slightest trace of guilt in the world. "These people out here—they've got nothing. I give them hope, don't you see? Even before the war and the collapse there were studies that showed that Western medicine was hardly more effective, if at all, than any belief system that a person felt was real and worked. Voodoo, faith healing, magnets around the wrists, pyramids over the head, owning a cat, getting inside a wooden box. You name it. Not only have people used these things but also they've gotten better through them. It's the mind that does the curing, Stone. It just needs a catalyst to make it do its thing. I give them that catalyst." He reached over and took a bottle of the amber liquid. "Snake oil contains no poisons; you can pour it on a wound and the alcohol will make a good antiseptic. Why, I even put ground-up tetracycline in this stuff to fight disease. Best of all," he said, leaning back and taking a swig, "you can get drunk on it.

Which, out here, may be the biggest blessing of all. Tell you the truth—I *do* drink a bottle every morning, and again before retiring."

"Oh, shit, give me a bottle too," Stone said, laughing. The man's logic and oratory skills were beyond his to debate. "You've convinced even me now. In fact, I think I'll take a gross for me and the dog."

"I'd like some too," a voice said gruffly from the front of the enclosure. Stone and the doctor turned in mid-gulp to see four men standing side by side, armed to the teeth. And they didn't look too friendly.

"Glad to oblige," Kennedy said as he edged slightly backward toward the shotgun he had hidden beneath the edge of the truck. Stone appeared not to move at all as the four heavily whiskered men approached, their hands hovering like birds around the pistols that bounced on their hips, but he shifted the jacket away from the holster on his hip so he could have quick access.

"Yeah, me and my brothers here," the man said, turning and waving his hand at the foul-smelling, poncho-wearing crew who accompanied him. They all looked like they hadn't had a bath since the war, had been sleeping in dirt, and hadn't washed, shaved, brushed their teeth, or used mouthwash for about as long. Stone could smell a revolting odor come from the mouth of their apparent leader, the largest of the four, who wore a black blanket, Indian-style, over his shoulders and chest. "We heard you had this here miracle medicine." The man laughed, feigning a cough and hitting at his chest. "Me and my brothers here all are sick and needs some of your magic snake oil."

"Glad to oblige." Dr. Kennedy smiled back, stepping inches closer to the truck. "I've got a good supply left, so I'm sure I can accommodate you. And in what form will you be making payment?"

"Payment?" The man looked momentarily surprised, as if he hadn't really thought about the question. Then his face broke into a wide grin as he stared straight into the snake oil man's eyes. "Payment will be in—"

Stone saw the motion first—the sudden movement underneath the thick black blanket that covered the man. Saw the ripple of motion toward the side. Only he was faster. His hand tore down to the huge Ruger .44 Blackhawk sitting on his hip and pulled it instantly free from the quick-draw holster as if it had been resting in air. He raised the long barrel just as the bearded man's pistol came free from beneath the long covering. Stone pulled the trigger of the mini-cannon, and it knocked his hand back a good three inches, even going with the recoil. The bearded face exploded as if a bomb had hit it, nose, ears, eyeballs, all sort of body parts heading off in different directions, followed by a spray of blood and brain tissue that filled the air.

Without hesitating, Stone turned the .44 mag to the right and sighted up another of the foul-smelling bastards just as the man's gun was rising toward his chest. Again Stone's Ruger erupted at the same instant the other man's did. His .45 bit into the side of the truck just behind Stone's shoulder, bending it in as if a steel tooth had tried to bite through. Stone's rifled .44 slug found its home in the man's stomach. The bullet tore in just above the abdomen and twisted a maze of bloody paths around inside, slicing liver and pancreas, kidney and intestine, into a thick red stew. The man's mouth spat out a whole cup of blood as his guts began dripping out onto the floor. Looking down, he staggered slowly backward, mumbling something to himself, staggered until he hit into the one of the tarp poles and then just fell to the ground, staring at his emptying innards.

The other two attackers had had their eyes on Dr. Kennedy, one with a .22 rifle, the other opening up with a cowboy-style Colt six-shooter. But the snake-oil man hadn't been around this long without picking up a few tricks. They had barely found him in their sights when he flicked his wrist and a cloud of green smoke rose all around him. The weapons fired straight into the cloud, but when it was blown away by the rising night breeze a few seconds later, the goateed, top-hatted man was nowhere to be seen.

"Here, boys, I believe it's me you're looking for." The two bear-sized mountain bandits turned, searching in the flickering air for the source. Suddenly their eyes just made contact with Kennedy, standing directly behind them, a derringer in each hand aimed straight at their faces.

"Bye-bye, boys," Kennedy said coolly, and pulled each trigger. Two eraser-sized holes appeared dead center in each of the foreheads. It hardly looked like anything was wrong or that anything had even happened. Just two little holes and two little trickles of blood that began flowing out. But it was enough. The bearded attackers just froze where they were. Froze forever, their faces looking most peculiar. Then they crumbled forward, falling together in perfect harmony that almost had a certain dancelike beauty to it, and landed side by side just outside the edge of the red-and-white-striped tarp where they lay face forward, their lips speaking only to the black dirt.

CHAPTER
Ten

THEY LEFT early the next morning, the bodies of their late-night attackers having been carted away—for which Dr. Kennedy had to pay a buck apiece to the town undertaker—to the local swamp where they were accorded all rights and then fed to the rats and the frogs. Although Kennedy knew the Certified Snake Oil was truly medicinal, the townsfolk might not see it that way when they woke up with a hangover as big as a tractor, their silver coins from their cookie jars missing. So the two men hit the road, driving slowly through the one-block-long metropolis just as the rising sun came up over a peak, lighting its icy crest with a halo of red that made the tower of granite look almost as if it were on fire, burning a welcome to the new day, a day like all others in post-nuke America, of blood.

Soon they were cruising along one of the best roads Stone had seen since he'd been out of the bunker. The highway was just beginning to crack, and Stone saw only a few of the skeleton families in their rusting automotive homes.

"I didn't even know this road existed," he said, elbow on the windowsill. Excaliber seemed more interested in goings-on today than in the previous few days and sat up between the two men on the seat, both front paws resting on the dashboard so that his head was just inches from the window. He watched every jackrabbit scurry off, every rustling of grouse feathers from behind stands of thick brush.

"I told you I knew a shortcut," the snake-oil salesman said. "This road isn't even on the maps. They never finished building it—it's a linkup from a north-south Colorado interstate to a north-south Utah interstate. Goes about two hundred miles and then stops dead as a doornail right in the middle of nowhere. But it will suit our purposes." As he spoke, with something of a Western twang in his voice today, the doctor kept pulling with one hand on the silver goatee, which he seemed to be greasing with some kind of oil that kept it white and shining.

"Tell me," Stone said, leaning around. "How fucking old are you, anyway? Every time I look at your face I don't know if you're twenty or ninety. I don't even know if your goatee is real, your silver hair real, or if the goddamned wrinkles on your face are real."

"And not for you to know. But *I* know one thing, friend," the doctor of snake oilology said, eyes glued to the road ahead. "They'll make mincemeat of you in the Resort. You just don't have a chance. This guy's heavy-duty, Stone. The stories I've heard about him would make your balls shrivel up into olives and your Adam's apple gong on your tonsils like a billiard ball. I mean—"

"I know what the bastard's capable of," Stone said softly. "And ordinarily I wouldn't care what he did or to whom he did it, but he's got my sister. Got her and—and there aren't any ands. I have no choice but to go after her. I'm sure you would do the same, were the roles reversed."

This time the goateed face was still, the mouth silent. Then after a few seconds he spoke. "Yes, I understand, beyond what you realize. Once I had someone. Someone I loved—my wife. I knew I would have only one woman in this life, and I had found her. But I was away for about a week from where we lived, and when I returned—" He was silent for almost a minute, then breathed out deeply, as if releasing all the cares of the world, and went on.

"I found out who did it—and I went after them. Oh, I went after them and found them too. Took my revenge. Revenge." He sighed. "It sounds sweet to the angry mind, but the taste is sour. Just more blood. Anyway, it didn't bring her back. And I knew I could love no other, so I've been roaming since, doing whatever it is that I do." The truck again went over a huge bump on the relatively flat four-lane highway, and the entire contents of the truck, every pin and every table, lifted a few inches and dropped down again, and the vehicle's suspension system groaned as if it were going to snap in two.

"All right, then, you've got to get in." Dr. Kennedy said. "But not like that. You'll need a disguise. I've got loads of them in the back. You'll be a gangster—a Mafia bigwig from the East Coast, here looking to buy drugs and women for a big whorehouse you're opening in New Jersey. You're going to have to be sharp in this place, Stone, like I told you. I can get you in, but after that..."

They drove on through the afternoon, Kennedy flooring the lumbering dinosaur of an overloaded vehicle, getting up to sixty miles an hour on the straightaways. The entire truck seemed to shift back and forth on its steel foundations, springs creaking like old floorboards. As the black night spread across the horizon like a bottle of spilled ink, meteors began streaking down through the darkness like dazzling jewels on a velvet easel. First one, then whole bunches of them, filled the skies, pouring down in a waterfall of fiery balls, some of them seeming to land just over the next rise, behind a near mountain. Excaliber watched them with wide, excited eyes, standing far forward in the seat, his eyes pressed right up against the glass as he stared skyward, barking with delight each time he spied one.

"Do you think we've poisoned it all, fucked up the whole planet?" Stone asked, almost rhetorically. "There seem to be more meteors, and they seem to come in lower, burn longer than I ever remember. Maybe part of the atmosphere is gone, the whole ecological system undergoing irreversible changes." Stone looked over to Kennedy, who seemed to be deep in thought or else just focusing totally on the road ahead, on which there were now more wrecks, more cars that must have been fleeing from the other direction when the first bombs went off, catching them, freezing them forever in its atomic sculptor's hands.

"I've seen a lot of strange things in my travels around the country, I'll tell you that," the doctor said, not pulling his eyes away for one second from the auto debris ahead, which was rapidly turning into an obstacle course of charred metal skeletons. "So you could be right. Either everything's dying—or it's all changing, twisting into something that can live. In any case I don't think you or I will be around a hell of a long time—so most likely we won't get to see the real results of all this mess when it comes down the pike."

"Cheerful thought," Stone said, his eye being caught by one of the unusually large flaming pieces of space boulder, which almost seemed to have dimensions to it as it came rolling in toward them like a small mountain on fire. It flew just over the nearest low peak, and this time there was a blast and flames that they could see lighting the mountains around them for a few seconds before dying out.

"Christ," Stone said, suddenly paranoically wondering if he'd end up being squashed beneath a meteor, crushed into a bloody, flaming pulp. What a way to go, killed by a chunk of galactic garbage that rolled down twelve million light-years of steps to hit you on the head.

"Shouldn't we stop for the night?" Stone asked at last, as they drove ever deeper into the darkening mountains, which began rising higher around them again as they entered some of the largest of the Utah range.

"No way—we're going all the way. Best to get there at night—when they're all drunk and drugged out—than in the light of day when they'll be feeling mean and examining visitors much more closely."

"Visitors?" Stone said. "What kind of visitors does this

place get exactly? I thought it was primarily the Dwarf's headquarters."

"The scum of the earth. The scum of the scum of the earth," Kennedy said with venom in his voice. "The heads of the Mafia, the motorcycle gangs, the warlords, the dope runners, and the gun dealers. All the people who now run America—really run it—since all federal and local government has collapsed. This is where they go to have fun— to let off some steam, to carry out their sick fantasies. The Dwarf runs the place like his private madhouse—orgies, opium dens, fighting games to the death. It's got everything that the mind of a pervert could conjure up—and more. Even the guards are insane in there. Dwarf brought them from the asylum, which had been blessed to be his place of residence for ten years before he made his escape. They're all mad as hatters—and totally loyal to him. That's why he uses them—outside help would surely assassinate him. All the crime bosses are in a constant state of trying to maneuver for power, always trying to make alliances with one another one minute and then trying to assassinate their partner the next. And they'd all love to get their hands on that armless and legless bastard who runs his part of the show with more brains and guts than any of them."

"You sound almost as if you like him," Stone said, letting his arm rest on top of Excaliber's head, who, now that the meteor shower was over, had grown bored and tired. Searching for a place to bed down, he nestled into Stone's thigh, letting the arm drop down on top of him as a blanket.

"Not like him—I hate him. I hate all those sick bastards. I'd love to see them dead. But I can't do anything against such odds. You'll see, soon enough, what you're up against. This isn't a bunch of guys with rifles standing in front of a barricade of tires. It might be a little more than you expect."

They had gone only another hour or so when, coming around a four-thousand-foot-high mountain pass and getting a sweeping view of the Utah landscape for a good fifteen miles ahead, Stone suddenly saw the retreat lit up in all its glory far below him, carved out of the solid side of a mountain. It must have been modeled on the Pueblo rock dwellings of New Mexico and farther south, for it had that primitive carved-into-the-wall look, but here, on an immense and spectacular high-tech scale.

The whole side of a twelve-hundred-foot-high granite mountain face had been blasted and hammered into shape—until it was a luxury vacation paradise made of steel and glass and sliding doors, and electric lights strung all across its hundred terraces that looked out over the valleys and the endless peaks off to the horizon. It was made up of numerous stories, multilevels, that rose above one another, straight up the side of the mountain. Elevators ran up and down the outside like crawling lanterned bugs, climbing and then dropping again slowly, depositing their passengers on the myriad floors. The whole thing seemed more like a mirage, a fairyland from the pages of an old book, than a real structure. Stone's jaw hung wide-open, as he just stared in a kind of horrified awe.

"Did dwarf—bui-build that?" Stone stuttered, hardly able to believe that from what he had seen, the technology existed today to carry out such an ambitious undertaking.

"No." Kennedy laughed. "No, it was a huge ski resort

in its prime, a hundred-million-dollar vacation paradise with hunting facilities, pools, ski lifts. Everything that the rich love to do most and that the poor suckers of America never even got to walk through the door of. It's the same now. Only Dwarf took it over. It's a haven for the sick, a getaway for the twisted, a week in the sun and snow for the perverts and sadists of America who get to act out the sickest of their fantasies and lose all their money in the gambling rooms and the arms of the thousand whores who work the place."

Stone took out a pair of binoculars from the pack he had planted on the floor, focused it on the place, and just stared and stared at the Christmas tree of lights that sparkled like the Milky Way. It wasn't a fucking fort—it was a city. A city that looked like it was filled with ten thousand people. Any ideas he'd been entertaining about being able to plant a few explosives, blowing out the side of a wall, or grabbing April and splitting, vanished like so many foaming bubbles flushing down a drain.

CHAPTER
Eleven

STONE HAD Kennedy drive them about a mile off the road after they reached the plateau that led to the Final Resort. They could see the shimmering oasis in the desert mountains that lay ahead and, even at that distance, they could hear the sounds of music, of many voices laughing and yelling . . . and screaming. Stone wanted to have a second escape option—rather than just the truck—in case something went wrong. And he couldn't take the dog. Its front left leg was still not at a hundred percent even though the pit bull seemed to be putting more and more weight on it each day. But the Dwarf had seen Stone with the dog back in Pueblo. Even with one of the snake doctor's disguises the pit bull would be a dead giveaway.

They found an extremely dense pack of woods on the slope of a small nearly hidden valley that looked as if no one had traversed it in years, not a trace of human garbage or slick of oil. The two men unloaded the war bike from the truck and wheeled it deep into the forest that was filled with the thousand sounds of night birds and stalkers. Excaliber ran off-balance circles around them on three legs, thinking it was all some sort of game. At last they had gone as far as the bike could possibly be squeezed and lay it on its side in the midst of some low bushes. Stone extracted the supplies he knew he would need for the operation and then covered the monster bike with grass and pieces of broken bush. After ten minutes it was virtually undetectable from even a few yards away.

He kneeled down beside the dog. "You're going to have to stay, dog. Okay, stay!" He pounded the ground with his hand and then pointed at the bike. "Guard bike! Stay bike—and guard! You understand?" The dog looked at him as if it understood but it didn't particularly like the idea.

"There's plenty of water in tin. See tin!" He pushed the dog's face toward a large five-gallon tin of water with the top cut off so the pit bull could get its face inside. "And here's some dried meat." Again Stone pointed toward five thick slabs of dried jerky that the dog loved to chew on and that would at least give it some nutrition for two or three days. And if it took longer than that, well, then Martin Stone wasn't coming back at all. The animal was on its own. He rubbed the pit bull's ears and then scratched its head hard. Then he stood up and pushed the creature's face, pointing it once more toward the motorcycle.

"Ah, the poor canine needs something more than a few quick pats," Dr. Kennedy said.

"Needs some Certified Snake Oil, he does." With that he pulled out a bottle of the stuff, opened it, and poured the entire contents into the animal's tin of water. Excaliber looked skeptically at the brown liquid mixing with the water in little rolling waves and took a tentative lick. Then he took another much deeper look and within a second or two was lapping away at the stuff with gusto.

The two men walked quickly away through the thicket of woods and brush. Stone kept looking back, but the animal stayed exactly where he had left it. It knew what he wanted. For the moment it would obey.

"You're going to have to change your image a little bit, my friend," Kennedy said when they got back to the truck, parked by the side of the back road, its lights out. "Come on." He jumped up onto the rear of the truck and opened a small door that was cut into the main metal one. They stepped inside, and Kennedy snapped on a light that ran off the truck's battery. Again Stone couldn't help but be amazed by the place. It was like a museum of the old world with collections of all its artifacts. If humanity ever did survive, as unlikely a prospect as that appeared, this one truck would tell them everything about their ancestors they could ever want to know.

The snake-oil salesman went over to an immense wooden chest and threw it open with a great heave. The inside was so filled with garments that it virtually exploded out, overflowing onto the floor. Suits, dresses, pirate outfits, leopard-skin sarongs, general's uniforms... "Where the hell is it?" Kennedy spat out impatiently as he literally flung clothes back over his shoulder so a whole pile of them waterfalled down onto the floor.

"Ah, here," he suddenly said with a shit-eating grin. He turned around holding a tailored suit, sharp creases still cutting the sides of the pants. Stone blanched. The thing was just about the most repulsive piece of menswear he had ever seen. It had shoulders that jutted out a good six inches past where his real shoulders would end on each side; wide, double-breasted lapels that flapped almost all the way to the other side of the chest like some oversized bird's wings; and huge, flopping bell-bottom-type pants—all in an almost luminous Pimp's Satin Pink color.

"You gotta be kidding?" Stone said, taking one look at the thing and feeling a little nauseated.

"This is what they're wearing these days. Believe me, I know." Kennedy smirked, enjoying Stone's discomfort. "You'll be in the height of fashion with this thing. Guys will be asking you for the name of your tailor. Don't give them mine." He laughed and handed Stone the shimmering suit. "I won it off a pimp in a dice game. He was an honest, though murderous, fellow—and stripped the damned thing off right on the spot and handed it to me. Looks like it'll fit you just fine."

"Forget it, mister," Stone said firmly. "No way, not a chance, not even a . . ."

Five minutes later Stone stood in front of a mirror with the pimp suit on, along with a pair of pointed, black patent-leather shoes; a yellow tie with what looked like little polka-dots of blood on it; and a pair of violet racing-style sunglasses that completely covered his eyes. He stared at himself long and hard and then turned to Kennedy.

"I'll tell you one thing, I don't look like the same blood-covered, black-leather-jacketed maniac who took out Pueblo."

"Uh-uh, pal, you got style now," Kennedy said, feeling proud of his couture creation. "Real style. Dare I say— you'll knock 'em dead."

But Stone had other thoughts as they drove down the last five hundred feet to the entrance of the mountainside resort. The size of the place was absolutely overwhelming. Windows and terraces just seemed to rise off in every direction, all filled with people.

The glass-enclosed elevators rushed up and down the side, taking guests to all the different facilities the place had to offer. Having been inside a cave, albeit a comfortable one, for five years, Stone had forgotten how big, how awe-inspiring man's technology had been, and what it had been capable of creating.

"How the hell does he keep the thing running?" Stone asked mystified, as the structure seemed so far ahead of everything else he had been seeing. Society was crumbling; most of the small shanty towns didn't even have electricity—let alone something of this magnitude. A metropolis in the middle of hell.

"The Dwarf's a genius, Stone," Dr. Kennedy said, adjusting his own red silk bow tie on the more laid-back black tux he had chosen to wear himself and, as always, his shining top hat. "Not just a genius of crime—but a genius of organization. He's managed to find technicians who can keep the whole show running. Has huge gasoline-powered generators, made from diesel truck engines in the subbasement, creates enough juice to run the whole fucking shebang."

Stone couldn't help but keep wondering if he had bitten

off just a bit more than he could chew. The concept of him taking on the man-made mountain of stone and steel that now towered over them as they approached the ovular, cave-like entrance that burrowed right into the base seemed laughable. Stone could see the guards now, everywhere, standing on terraced emplacements all around the lower levels of the place, armed with machine guns and even small artillery. They could take on an army from here, Stone thought. The place was more than a fortress, it was an impregnable citadel.

The truck slowed as they approached the tunnel, red lights blinked slowly on and off, and a beam of metal blocked their way like a gate at a railroad crossing. Two of the guards walked over from behind sandbagged emplacements behind which dozens of them lounged around, trying to stay warm. They were odd-looking to say the least, every man dressed exactly the same—blue ski parka and pants; high, black leather boots that came up nearly to the knee and narrow-slitted ski-racing sunglasses so that you could hardly see their eyes. They all carried the same weapon dangling on leather straps around their shoulders—Thompson sub-machine guns with immense, round magazines ready to spray out a death storm of .45 slugs.

"Name?" the guard on the driver's side asked Kennedy.

"Dr. Abraham Reagan Kennedy," he replied. "Here for the Dwarf's Holiday Spectacular. I come every year. The magician, remember?" He reached up and appeared to take a card from the guard's ear. But the blue-wool-capped guard didn't seem to like the idea.

"Don't you be taking nothing from my face," the man said, raising his heavy automatic weapon up to waist level.

"Sorry, sorry." Kennedy smiled, making the card disappear just as quickly. He had forgotten how touchy the insane could be.

"I got things trying to take my face," the guard mumbled beneath his breath. "They come at night—rip the flesh. They—like blood."

"Yes, I'm sure." Kennedy smiled. "I'm sure they do. Now, please, if we could move on, get inside. I have a lot of setting up to do for the Dwarf's party. I'm sure you wouldn't want me to be late, wouldn't want to upset him." The guard leaned forward and looked over at Stone.

"Who's he?" he asked suspiciously.

"He's my assistant magician." Kennedy smiled again, trying to keep the jittery guard, who kept fingering the Thompson nervously, relaxed and in a relatively peaceful state of mind. "He's just learning all the tricks of the trade so he can carry on when I'm gone."

"Does he make things rise from the face?" asked the guard, whose eyes were totally shielded from view by the wide, impenetrable glasses—just a hint of white peering from within the narrow slits.

"No, he's not into faces," Kennedy reassured the man. "Just ropes and dogs."

"All right, all right, go ahead through," the guard said suddenly losing patience with the whole situation. He waved them through, and another guard about ten feet away pulled a lever and the steel beam lifted creakily up.

"They're called 'the Mad'—the guards, that is," Kennedy

said as they drove slowly through the brilliantly lit tunnel. "That's the Dwarf's designation for them, anyway. Only to him its an accolade, a term of respect. He believes, if I understand him correctly, that only the insane are normal— that the sane are locked in tombs within their own minds. The mad, on the other hand—those like himself—can see beyond, into the realms that mortal man is not normally privy to. Be careful of them. They're unpredictable, dangerous as hell."

"Seems like a strange choice to be guards, to carry weapons like that," Stone said.

"That's the way Poet likes it," Kennedy said. "It adds a certain existential what's-going-to-happen-next quality that he seems to thrive on. Part of the charm of the place apparently is that you don't ever know for sure if you'll be alive from minute to minute. Thrills, Stone, thrills. That's all they're looking for here."

They came through the tunnel and into an immense courtyard the size of two football fields around which automobiles were parked—Lincolns, Rolls-Royces, even a Jaguar or two—cars that Stone hadn't imagined still existed. On the walkways that rose all around them as high as the eye could see, crowds of people were walking—primarily ugly, bull-necked, nasty-looking fellows with Neanderthal-featured faces, around whom hordes of young women hovered, like ants around sugar. Many of the women's breasts were exposed, dancing like nectar-filled gourds in the night air; others wore costumes so skimpy, one could see everything that one might want. As Stone took in more and more of the place he saw that many of the men had their hands cupped around the breasts, buttocks, or other curved flesh of their escorts. In some of the doorways women on their knees serviced the stiffened tools of their charges.

"Boy, they don't hold back here." Stone laughed as Kennedy drove the truck off to one side of the wide, octagon-shaped courtyard that literally had been dug out of the side of the mountain. Far above, Stone could see the clouds rolling by, like the foaming lips of the sky, melting into one another in a dark embrace.

"No, they don't believe in repression of the libido at the Final Resort." Kennedy grinned. The motto here is: Whatever you can think—do! Dwarf runs an open ship. And I mean open. That's nothing," Kennedy said, sweeping his hand at the casual sex scenes being played out on all the terraces and walkways that surrounded them, sparking with a rainbow of lights. "That's just appetizer."

CHAPTER
Twelve

THEY LEFT the truck, and Kennedy led Stone through the courtyard. An immense fountain shot out from the very center of the open court, twin geysers, a yard wide, and reaching fifty feet in the air where they arched and splashed back down into the round catch basin. The water was red. Deep blood-red, so it looked as if the very Earth itself was bleeding, shooting its innards into the night sky, towering fountains of red lit up from three sides by spotlights so they glistened and shimmered, as the blood seemed to bubble at the top, evaporating in a pink mist that rose up past the multilevels filled to overflowing with "tourists." As they drew closer to the twenty-foot-wide catch basin Stone nearly gagged—for floating belly up in the swirling red water were fish, hundreds of them, dead and bloated, mock-swimming as they were pulled this way and that by the currents.

"Guy's got a great sense of humor," Stone muttered to Kennedy.

"He bases his philosophy on a mixture of the writings of the Marquis de Sade, Zen Buddhism, and Nietzschean nihilism—or so he told me at our last encounter," Kennedy related to Stone as they made their way up some stairs, hand-carved in the granite, and up to the main entrance. A doorman, another blue nylon parkaed member of the Mad, opened an immense brass door for them and spoke.

"Welcome to the Final Resort," the expressionless face said, "where dreams come true. All dreams—dreams born in heaven, dreams born in hell. Whatever you desire, desire most foul, from the darkest parts of your soul—it is here. You can have it." The mouth of the doorman moved, but the face didn't. It was like they were all under some kind of mental control, drugged or lobotomized. Stone had never seen someone so unconnected to his own will. The voice went on for a few more seconds like an automatic recording, ending with, "Please register straight ahead at the desk." Then it stopped, the mouth almost seeming to click off as the stone face turned away from them and back toward the door, and the doorman's body fell into a limp attention, expending zero energy until it was time to move again.

They walked through the immense main lobby with its marbled floors, mirrored walls, and overhead, high-tech chandeliers hanging like mini-suns pouring down a flood of light. Gangsters, bikers, mountain bandits, any scum, no matter how high or low his station, who had the bucks could get in here—and have his fun.

"Yes, gentlemen," a voice said pleasantly from behind the long, curved mahogany counter. An obese woman the size of a small car sat behind the counter on a wide stool.

Her face was smiling and pleasant enough, but the body was so fat that folds of the white flesh seemed just to hang from her face, her neck, everywhere, as if she were made of soft dough. She weighed in at an easy four hundred pounds, Stone guessed as she smiled at them, and even her fat lips seemed to quiver like little tubes of red Jello. "How may I be of service to you?"

"Like two rooms," Kennedy said, taking off his ever-present top hat and resting it on the counter. "Believe you have a reservation for me—name of Kennedy. I'm here to perform for the Dwarf's Christmas pageant."

"Kennedy, Kennedy." She rifled through a stack of file cards that sat in front of her and pulled out one. "Yes, it's here. You have the Capone Suite, on level ten, overlooking the courtyard—a beautiful room. The Dwarf must hold you in high regard."

"Yes, we've had our moments," Kennedy said, poker-faced. "But what about my traveling companion here, Vito 'Pimp' Staloni," Kennedy said, glancing over at Stone, who bowed and smiled as lasciviously as he could from within the pink pimp suit that positively glowed beneath the luminescent fixtures that blazed down from above. "His car was attacked by bandits about eighteen miles back," Kennedy said, leaning forward on the counter so he could get a good look at where all the keys and personal items were kept. "Killed his chauffeur and two of his bodyguards. Man barely got away with his life. Can you believe it? Right in the Dwarf's own territory! If I hadn't come barreling down the road right then, I don't know what would have happened." The immense woman reached with dainty fingers—

nails inches long and colored with a lustrous black enamel—down in front of her and slowly, as if touching the most precious object in the universe, lifted a chocolate candy to her mouth and deposited it between the wriggling red lips, all the time looking sympathetically at Stone.

"Yeah, we've been having a lot of trouble lately with these sons of bitches who attack our clientele," she said, half coughing as she swallowed the sugary load. "Dwarf has been talking about sending out a search-and-destroy operation to wipe out these bloodsucking rats once and for all. But I will most certainly notify him of the attack on your party, Mr. Staloni, and I'm sure that this will be the straw that broke the bandit's back, so to speak."

She reached for another candy and poked it into the grinding red hole of a mouth. "And may I say, on behalf of the staff of the Final Resort, how sorry we are for any inconvenience that may have been caused you. Let me give you room 2213—one of the best bridal suites, at the very top level of the hotel, with a view of half of Northern Utah, sunken bathtub, Jacuzzi . . . and lots more." She winked so that one of the clamshell-size eyes slapped hard against the other and then opened up, staring straight at Stone with undeniable lust in her heart, her lips parted just so, with a little rim of moisture formed at the edges. Stone looked away in horror.

With a loud sigh she dropped the pose and clapped her hands hard so that the fat beneath the hanging folds of her blue satin dress and the huge chair-sized breasts rolled around like things alive. Two smooth-faced teens appeared from out of nowhere wearing traditional bellhop gear and even little brimless caps circa 1920. The Dwarf obviously spared no expense in paying attention to his own weird concepts of hotel aesthetics.

"Now these boys will take you to your rooms, gentle-men—and then it's up to you. We offer incomparable services—of every kind. You will be billed at the end of your stay—cost is a thousand dollars per day. And that includes everything—room, food, alcohol, sex, drugs. Ordinarily we would demand a cash deposit of at least three thousand dollars, but seeing as how you're Mr. Kennedy's friend, we'll toss all that. I can tell by your dress and manner that you're both men of high standing—and breeding." She looked down at Stone's crotch area and then ran the very tip of her pointed tongue along the shiny red lips. "Gambling rooms are on levels seventeen to twenty; drinking and drug rooms, fifteen and sixteen; sex and orgy rooms are on ten to fourteen. The death games run from five to nine, and the standard sports and recreations are on main floor to the fourth."

She looked bored now and recited the litany as she had ten thousand times before as she filed away at a chipped edge of pinky nail with quick, violent strokes. "There are also dance floors on the main floor, twelfth floor—and, of course, the roof garden. Girls, boys, and transsexuals can be ordered at any time for private pleasure in your own rooms. Merely pick up the phone by your bed and specify your request. Please have sex, age, and other vital information ready when placing your order."

She suddenly stopped in her tracks and looked at both of them. "Ah, hell, you guys know what you want. Half the assholes who come in don't even know how to lift up a phone." She caught Stone's eye again. "Hey, Mr. Staloni, if you get tired of those skinny bags of bone upstairs and want a big woman who can fuck all night, I'm in room 107. Get off about four. Anytime!" She glared down at the two teenage bellhops, who reached for Stone's and Kennedy's luggage, lurching off under the heavy loads toward the bank of elevators to the right.

The two men agreed to meet later in the main gambling room, and the snake-oil doctor got off at his floor while Stone shot up in the glass elevator with such speed that his stomach felt like it was constantly about twenty feet behind. From within the glass cage of the glowing sphere that crawled up the side of the mountain, passing level after level of pleasure seekers, Stone could slowly see the Utah landscape come into view as they rose past the lower peaks ahead. Suddenly the elevator seemed to scrape along its casings with a loud, nerve-shattering sound like chalk being dragged along a chalkboard, and the entire booth slammed back and forth like a gong inside a bell.

The bellhop acted like nothing untoward had happened. Evidently there were little flaws in the Dwarf's techno paradise. The doors opened on the top level, and the hop led the way down the hallway. On closer inspection, everything looked a little frayed, Stone realized as the teen led him around a long, curved walkway from which he could look out for miles. The astroturf carpeting was worn in many places and stained with red. Some of the frames that held the windows in place within granite walls were coming loose, twisting out of shape so that the glass was curving out, ready to snap free.

Suddenly Stone almost tripped as he had been looking up to see what else was falling down. He looked down, grabbing for his balance on the four-foot fence that ran along the perimeter of the outdoor walkway. It was a body, a woman's, naked, her face and chest covered with blood. She had been mutilated, horribly. Stone had to look away.

"Did—did you see that?" he asked the hop incredulously as the lad stood about ten yards ahead, looking back impatiently.

"Yes, I did, sir," said the boy, who couldn't have been more than twelve or thirteen with cream-colored, youthful skin but dark, heavily circles eyes, purple bruises below them. Eyes that looked as if they'd seen hell. "And I'll notify the cleanup squad first thing after I get you all squared away," the youth said with that same monotone voice that just about everyone in the place had, as if their very willpower had been whipped out of them so that they were like old beaten dogs, ready to accept any punishment or carry out any command.

"But—she—she's dead," Stone said, not understanding the hop's bored reaction.

"Lot's of em is dead. Die all the time here, mister. Sometimes ten, even twenty a night if the gentlemen is partying hard. I mean, they *are* here for your pleasure, aren't they, sir?" the lad asked, lifting the bags again as if to say, *Please let's get going*. Stone stumbled mutely after him, looking back at the already hardening corpse of the young female. Rigor mortis had pulled her arms up in a contorted position so it almost looked as if she were trying to cover her bloody breasts, or the holes where they once had been. Even as she lay moldering, her cold cells were hardening into a protective shield to give her some dignity in the hideousness of her death.

"Here we are, sir," the hop said with as enthusiastic a sound as he could muster. He slid the large key into Stone's lock and pushed the door open, stepping inside and flicking the switch on the wall. Stone gasped at the expanse of fabrics and colors, of Persian rugs and gold-fringed draperies that met his eyes. It was like the room of an emperor, a luxury for the senses. The hop showed him around the three-room suite—the satin-sheeted bed with mirrors overhead, the cable TV with pornographic films of every conceivable taste able to be called up, the private bar, the blue-veined marble bathroom with golden faucets and soap dish.

"And last but not least," the hop said on his way out, "the rack for tying and punishing your sex toys." He walked over to the living room wall and pulled a handle to a built-in floor-to-ceiling wooden unit. The whole wall seemed to come out, like a Murphy bed, and the unit opened up as it came down, revealing all kinds of ingeniously built-in torture equipment that popped up, ready for use. A rack, a cross for crucifixions, a chair with chains—all the little things that added to life's pleasure.

"Huh, thanks," Stone said numbly as the hop walked to the door and opened it.

"Here's your key, sir," he said, dropping the long key into Stone's hand. The lad just stood and stared at him without moving until at last, feeling like an idiot, Stone reached into his pocket and took out a silver dollar and handed it to the youth. The hop took it, and his eyes opened wide, his mouth widening into a grin, the first real expression of any kind of pleasure Stone had seen the boy make.

"Thanks, mister," the hop said as he stepped through the doorway. "And listen—watch out. Watch out a lot."

CHAPTER
Thirteen

"**W**ATCH OUT a lot," Stone mumbled to himself as he looked around the place. It wasn't even good English. But it had the desired effect of making him feel ... nervous. Were there video cameras, microphones? His eyes darted around, searching for telltale signs of human intervention—but it was impossible to discern anything, as the place was so filled with expensive fabrics and nude sculptures of men and women in intimate forms of embrace. He was feeling more unnerved by the minute, positively intimidated by everything about the place.

He walked to the wide picture window through which faint stars poked here and there as the cloud cover thinned just a little, and stared out at the mountains cutting south through the black night like the scales of a dragon. Stone could see tiny flashes of light—fires from little bands of men trying to protect themselves from the night's dangers. Yet here, in the midst of all the light and silk pillows in the world, Martin Stone gladly would have traded places with them in an instant to be out of this palace of sickness.

He checked his Uzi and the huge Ruger on his hip, making sure they were basically hidden by the huge, tentlike folds of the pink pimp suit—the only thing he would admit to liking about it. Then he headed out. Stone could hardly believe the place as he walked down the slowly sloping ramps that connected terrace to terrace. He stopped on each floor, walking through the myriad "party rooms" to see what they contained and to try to find even the slightest clue as to April's whereabouts.

If there was a Sodom and Gomorrah on the face of the earth, this was it. Floor after floor of luxuriously appointed, ultramodern decor, thick plush carpeting—everything designed for the pleasure of the flesh, of the jaded senses. Girls filled the place like schools of darting fish, until they got snagged by this or that gold-ringed dark fist and pulled down into the darkness to join in whatever brand of fun was happening in the shadows. Drugs were sold everywhere by women clad in G-strings with little pills for pasties on the ends of their nipples. They had everything one could put into a nervous system—ups, downs, tranquilizers, barbiturates, hallucinogenics, opiums, magic mushrooms, and the purest of cocaines and heroins, arranged in perfect straight lines on silver trays. One could sniff, eat, or shoot up, as hypodermic needles lay neatly arranged along one side of the tray, cocked and ready to go.

The S&M chambers were the worst, and he could only force himself to go on by telling himself it was for April's sake; everything was for her. Young girls were roped up on racks, revolving before their appreciative audiences of red-faced men. The girls spun slowly, their perfect nakedness revealed in all their innocence and vulnerability, as whips flashed out of the shadows and ripped into that soft flesh, leaving little gouges behind, little rivulets of blood that streaked down their firm breasts.

Each room held its own particular brand of torture—from spanking to paddling to whipping—then on to the more "sophisticated" fun: piercing with needles and nails; hanging slowly, exquisitely tortured to death by suffocation, by soft silk ropes as coarse male faces peered close to see the death spasms, hands moving in quick, jerking motions below. And others—pierced by phalluses made of iron and stone, objects so large that they were literally split apart as the things were slowly, inexorably driven deeper into them; cold, alien lovers of unimaginable pain. Sometimes death took hours, even days. Women at the Final Resort were totally disposable, like razors had been in the prewar days. Squeezed to the last bloody drop of whatever pleasure they could provide their sick audiences—and then thrown away, like pieces of garbage.

Stone felt tears fill his eyes as he saw how young some of the girls were. He had the strongest urge to reach for his pistols and begin blazing away, just getting as many of the sick bastards as he could. But he knew it would be to no avail. He would be gunned down in seconds—and April, along with all the others, would die. "Control, Martin," the Major had always said, "is the only thing that differentiates man from the barbarian. It's worth more than a thousand guns."

But it was hard. The girls kept reminding him of April, the same young faces, bodies hardly old enough to have scars on them—but the eyes all like those of the bellhop in his room, filled with a terror beyond terror, a terror that wished only to die and to be taken out of its living hell. And Stone looked, too, into the eyes of the killers, the thugs, the drug-crazed bikers, the drug dealers, the Mafia torpedos, the hard-faced pimps who watched it all in an intoxicated bliss of infinite degradation. And their eyes were as dead as cold rocks, filled with only a vacuum where a soul should be.

Not finding April anywhere, which he was just as relieved about, and unable to stand the screams and the scent of hot blood, Stone headed down to the gambling rooms where Kennedy had arranged to meet him. The main room was a huge affair with arched cathedral ceilings lit with a bank of fluorescent lights that ran along each side and down the center, positively inundating the place with a blinding illumination. The room was filled with the smell of sweat and cigar smoke as voices screamed out numbers or rolled down dice with shouts of encouragement from their tossers. Everywhere Stone turned, money flew like leaves in a storm, as twisted faces partook of the frenzy of no-holds-barred gambling.

Here and there an occasional disagreement flared up between this or that immense gorilla-shouldered vacationer. Ham-size fists would fly, or a knife flash in the brilliant air. And another body would be taken away by the cleanup squad. And that was that. No complaints, no problems, no lawsuits, everything settled on the spot—and fast. But then, the frequenters of the Final Resort wouldn't have it any other way.

Stone tried to listen in on all the passing bits of conversation he heard. Anything, any bit of information, could lead to April—and maybe a way to take out this whole damned cesspool. He heard them all. Heard them spill their guts without even realizing it, for they were all drunk and drugged and filled with the weary look of sexual overdose. Heard their drug deals and their sordid double crosses of their pals, heard them planning assassinations, takeovers, robberies, and just where old so-and-so's body had actually been tossed. All the gossip of murder.

Stone stopped behind five very well-dressed men, all dandied out in custom-tailored duds, who stood in front of a large roulette wheel. He pretended to be looking the other way, absolutely disinterested in them or their conversations.

"Girls—" he heard one man say. Then, "We need at least a hundred for the West Coast."

"Man, you know what I can get for a good young white bitch," the man to the immediate right of Stone said with a laugh. "Ten times what I'll pay here. The demand is outrageous. It's a seller's market right now. I tell you, I could unload a goddamned freighter full of good disease-free female meat."

"Well, you're going to have to bid against me," a towering man with shoulders that looked as wide as a car said, off to Stone's other side. "'Cause I have orders I *have* to fill. The radiation's destroyed the fertility of so many women east of the Mississippi that breeding bitches with rad-free chromosomes are worth their weight in gold. And from what

Dwarf has been saying, every one of the batch he's selling off tomorrow is certified radiation-free—with official seal and all."

The speaker turned suddenly and bumped into Stone's shoulder so that his own drink sloshed all over his pants.

"Hey, watch it, pal. What the hell's wrong with you?" the seven-footer shouted at Stone, who shrugged, stepping past him as if he had just been about to come to the roulette wheel.

"Hey, yeah, sorry about that, pal," Stone said, smiling with ivory teeth at the lug as he ran his finger beneath his nose, as if he had just been sniffing cocaine. The man glared at him for a few seconds and then, not in the mood to spill blood unless he had to, turned back to his own group. Stone looked up at the roulette wheel as the huge spinning disk whirred rapidly around in the air. A red-and-black ball was bouncing from slot to slot as the wheel began decelerating. Stone watched, wondering why the ball seemed to bounce so unevenly. And then he saw—it wasn't a ball, it was a head. A human head, the mouth still stretched out in the most terrified look of horror that Stone had ever seen. The eyes were somehow preserved in the otherwise shriveled face, and they stared out as the head, cut right at the top of the neck and sealed off with plastic so the thing made a rough ball, came to a stop, caught in a red slot, number 29.

"That's mine, that motherfucker is mine," a Guardian of Hell with black jacket and chains draped over him yelled out, slamming his fist down on the table.

"House pays twenty-nine," the spinner called out in a

nasal voice. He pushed a pile of coins over to the biker, who embraced the winnings as if they were a long-lost lover.

"I was broke." The biker smiled, catching Stone's eye, standing a few feet away from him. "Now I can get high again—and buy more pussy. Oh, lord, let me die having the ultimate orgasm." He swept the winnings into his unraveling pockets and headed out the door to one of the sex floors. Stone took out a five-dollar silver piece and placed it down on the number 33, his lucky number since he had been just a kid, for no particular reason that he could remember.

"Place your bets. Last chance," the spinner yelled, taking the head out from the bottom of the wheel, lifting it by the hair. The thing had been drained of all its blood long ago, but occasionally some of the undried brain tissue inside would ooze out of the ears like wax, and the spinner would take out a handkerchief and clean the thing's ears, looking inside them to make sure they weren't moist. He took pride in his work and would not allow any uncleanliness.

He reached up and gripped the wheel around the edge, jumped in the air, and came down, pulling the immense disk with all his strength. It instantly whirled into a blur, all the numbers and colors melting together in a soupy rainbow.

"Around she goes, around she goes, where she stops nobody knows." The spinner grinned out at the thirty or so men who stood pressed around the table, eyes glued to the wheel. When he felt the speed was just right, he heaved the head up and inside where it crashed off the inner wall of the wheel and began bouncing wildly around, completely asymmetrically, as by no stretch of imagination was it actually round.

"Seven, seven," the man who had bumped him yelled out a few yards away. "Come on, little baby, come on, sweet seven, come home to Daddy."

"Come on, thirty-three," Stone coughed out, trying to get into the spirit of things. The head continued to fly around, the ghastly eyes occasionally staring out for just a split second, as if the thing were looking straight at him. Then it would roll on again, never at rest, never at peace.

"Seven, man, I want seven," the hulking fellow yelled louder, glancing over at Stone as if to say shut up.

"Come on, thirty-three," Stone just couldn't resist yelling again as the head started rolling to a stop, the mouth turning over and over as if trying to kiss the air. At last it rolled to a standstill. Thirty-three. It was just feet away from Stone, the full front of the face tilted right at him. He swore he could feel something in those eyes, something trying to scream out behind those lips. He looked away quickly.

"Bank pays number thirty-three," the house banker yelled, pushing over Stone's winnings with a long croupier's pole.

"My number was seven," the hulk said with a very unhappy scowl, staring over at Stone, who counted his fifty-to-one return.

"Sorry about that," Stone said as he looked up at the man. "Try another number next time. Try thirty-three, for example."

"Hey, look here, we got us a wise asshole." The man laughed, instantly reverting to his street ways and wiping his nose with the sleeve of a thousand-dollar silk suit. The others in the party turned, and Stone took in the full force of their combined venomous hate and pure, dark wills. Stone could see immediately that the middle two were the powers, the rest just their henchmen. They radiated decadence, greased faces that had seen everything, eyes that had condemned men to death again and again without the slightest flicker of mercy.

They stood side by side, contrasts in their own dark style. The taller one wore a dark blue, almost subtle, pin-striped suit. He was covered with diamonds—in his lapel and on his fingers—and looked almost as large as the gorilla who was coming toward Stone like he wanted to take his head off. The other was much shorter, with an almost boyish, but ratlike, face. He had a narrow Sicilian mustache and thin white lips that made the rodent impression even stronger, and he wore a spotless white silk suit and white gloves. Even from yards off, Stone could smell the numerous colognes the man wore, and from the way his eyes ran up and down Stone's thighs the man's sexual preferences were as twisted as the rest of the place.

"What's the problem?" the white-suited one asked, whipping out an embroidered handkerchief and rubbing it around his face, wiping the beads of sweat that stood out on his head.

"No problem, boss," said the gorilla, who had stopped about three feet from Stone and was staring at him as he cracked the knuckles of both hands. "Just that this asshole won and I didn't."

"Sounds like a good reason, don't it, Scalagi." The diamond-cluttered mafioso laughed, elbowing his smaller companion in the ribs.

"Where are you from, asshole?" the cologned one asked Stone, looking him full in the face and sending out a stare like the fat woman had downstairs. Everyone wanted to either kill him or sleep with him. Or both.

"I'm from the East Coast, asshole," Stone snapped back as the white-suited man's bodyguards shifted uneasily on each side at the insult and reached into their jackets. "Name's Staloni. They call me Vito 'Pimp' Staloni. From Jersey City, the Port," Stone lied, praying none of them this far west would have been that far east. The two bosses looked at each other and shrugged their shoulders.

"Never heard of you, asshole," the diamond-studded one said with a laugh.

"Never heard of you either, asshole," Stone replied, his eyes as dark and impenetrable as an artic ice floe. One of the guards laughed nervously, as if he found the tense exchange humorous, but the smaller, white-suited one didn't find it amusing at all.

"Only difference is, asshole," the dandy said, dabbing the scarf around his face as if to keep Stone's odor away from him, "that we're important assholes—and you're just a peon asshole from the sewer. So you ain't worth shit." The big torpedo who had betted against Stone smiled, as he took the words to mean that he could take Stone out. He rushed forward suddenly, trying to catch the much smaller man off-balance, cocking his immense hand back, purple knuckles broken from a thousand fights.

He threw a right hook that could have taken the head off

a mule. Only Martin Stone wasn't a mule and hadn't trained all those years in hand-to-hand combat with the Major in their mountain fantasy world without learning something. As the punch came in, he leaned inside it and came up with a knee to the man's groin. The huge body stopped as if a lightning bolt had struck it, and the big, puffed lips opened wide, issuing a howl of pain. The torpedo hobbled around for a few seconds as the others looked on, amused by the fight. Some of the other gamblers stopped their betting and turned to watch. A fight was always better than cards— and it took their minds off their losses.

"Motherfucker, you shouldn't have done that," the huge torpedo said, catching his breath and rising up straight. He reached into his jacket and pulled out a meat hook, a long, curved number with rusting point that still looked sharp enough to slam right through a steer, or a man's throat, and hang him on a wall. He swung the foot-long hook through the air, making quick circles, and laughed looking at the others of his party, who were amused by the turn of events.

"I think I'll get a little exercise," he said, going into a crouch and starting toward Stone. "I been doing so many drugs and so much fucking, I can't hardly move. Ain't killed for over a week."

"That long?" Stone said, clicking his lips together in mock sympathy. "It's only been a few days for me, but one does miss it so." He reached inside the double-breasted pink pimp jacket and pulled out a push dagger, a knife with a blade that popped out in the center. The handle fit snugly in his hand, the blade protruding forward from between his middle fingers. Stone went into a boxing stance, arms loose, moving on his toes.

The giant, with a half-dead yellow carnation pinned to his lapel, came forward suddenly, whipping the meat hook all over the place, trying to tear into Stone's chest. But his would-be victim was faster. He stepped sharply to the side, out of range of the blur of steel, and then threw his left hand, holding the push dagger with its six-inch blade forward, with a sudden snap, and then back. The narrow but razor-sharp knife edge slipped right into the man's carotid artery in the side of his throat, cutting it cleanly in two. A torrent of blood instantly began pulsing out from the wound.

Not even realizing that he had been stabbed and had only seconds left to live, the torpedo turned with a grunt and started forward again, this time raising the meat hook like a club about to descend and tear Stone's brains into hell. But again, the much younger and swifter man threw his hand out, twice, three times, in quick, boxing jabs. And with every punch the knife blade hidden between his fingers tore into the side of the man's throat and under his chin.

Stone stepped back . . . and waited. Now the torpedo knew something was wrong. He tried to move, but nothing was happening. Suddenly he felt a strange sensation on his neck and chest, beyond the drink he had spilled earlier, and looked down. The gasp of horror on even his hardened face was not dissimilar to that frozen scream on the human ball in the roulette wheel, for all he was, from the neck down, was red. Thick gushes of blood pumped from all four slices in the thick neck, pumped like water from a fire hydrant, pouring out over the floor. In ten seconds half his blood was gone. The wide, battered face turned whiter and whiter as all the blood drained from the brain. And then the bodyguard tried to walk forward toward his bosses but only managed to do a funny little dance before he fell forward, face smashing into the side of a craps table, the metal-edged corner cracking right through the skull of the corpse so it bounced back and crashed down onto its side, sending blood and brain membrane over the pants of the two bosses.

The white-suited one stared down at himself, his favorite suit, the one that made him feel "beautiful" splattered with red. A thousand dots and drips and streaks of the stuff that still gushed from the neck of his bodyguard of ten years. The two other torpedos started in earnest for the firepower they had concealed under their jackets, but the diamond-fingered one stopped them.

"No, not here, not now! It could be a trap," the sweat-shining face said breathlessly. "Let's get out of here." The entire group turned and headed toward the door, not even deigning to look back at the pitiful carcass they left behind, its head now so saturated with its own red blood that it no longer even looked human but like something out of a nightmare, something primeval and infinitely ugly.

"You're dead meat, Mr. Tough Man Staloni," the white-suited mafioso hissed in a mock effeminate manner. "Fuck everyone and everything you can tonight—because tomorrow you die!"

CHAPTER
Fourteen

"OUT OF the way, corpse coming through," the cleanup crew of four yelled out as they came running through the crowd with a wheelbarrow. They grabbed hold of the totally limp body, as white as a sheet, and hefted it up into the wheelbarrow where it collapsed in a crumpled heap. They jumped up just as quickly as they'd come and headed out again. Within a minute a cleaning woman walked over, got down on her knees, and scrubbed away at the floor with brush and detergent, trying to get the stains. They knew how to deal with death quickly and efficiently at the Final Resort—with the least amount of mess possible.

"That was really stupid," a voice whispered in Stone's ear as the crowds, now bored with the event, got back to their gambling. Stone turned, the knife still gripped in his fist, ready to deal out more death punches.

"Easy, easy," the voice said, resting a hand on his shoulder. It was Kennedy.

"Sorry, Doc," Stone said, wiping the blade free of blood on a napkin, then folding it and putting it back in his jacket. "I get a little weird when I fight, when I kill. Go into a different frame of mind. It takes me a minute to come out."

"Do you know who those guys were that you just tangled with there?" Kennedy asked with rising inflection.

"Obviously someone important or your eyebrows wouldn't be touching your forehead." Stone scowled. "Why don't you tell me, I'm just dying to know."

"That was Tough Tony Valenzi—the guy with the shitload of diamonds—and the mincing one, that was Pretty Boy Scalagi. You may not have heard of them, but since we ain't got no more U.S. government, those guys are probably among the top twenty most influential motherfuckers in America. I mean, these guys have their own armies. They're traveling light here—'cause they're vacationing—but to-morrow, all they're going to want to do is find you and see what you sound like when you scream."

"What can I say?" Stone said, shrugging his shoulders and again feeling unconsciously for his guns. At least he had something, something that could put up a fight against the bastards when they came for him.

"Listen, I'm not backing out of helping you or anything," Kennedy said, suddenly looking around as if he felt eyes on him. "I swear—but—we better act like we don't know each other. I'll be more help to both of us if I'm not con-nected up to you. Things could get rough. Be careful, Stone. Be real careful." With that, the snake-oil man was gone, disappearing into the crowd. That was the second time in an hour that people had told him to be careful. As if he had a choice. As if everybody and everything wasn't trying to kill him already.

"That was beautiful," a soft voice spoke, breaking into his momentary fog of paranoia.

"What was beautiful?" Stone asked, turning to see the face of a full-bodied and extremely beautiful blonde, with breasts the size of ripe grapefruits, pressing toward him.

"The way you killed." The woman laughed, throwing her long, shimmering hair over her shoulder. "It turned me on."

"Oh." Stone gulped, not quite sure of the correct witty repartee to the statement.

"Yes, I do hope that doesn't shock you," she went on, pressing closer to Stone so that he could feel the heat of her flesh against his arm. "Men who are strong and able to kill other men—it does something to me. Arouses something deep inside me. And you were so swift and efficient. I don't think most of them even knew what occurred out on that floor. But I do. It was ... beautiful."

She moved toward him so that he couldn't have avoided her even if he wanted to, and put her arms around his waist so that her whole chest was pressing up against him.

Her breasts felt so hot that they would surely explode at any moment, the hard nipples poking against him, forcing his body to respond with desire. And after a few seconds it did. Stone felt his senses swoon with a sudden deep, physical desire. Her perfume filled his nostrils like an aphrodisiac, her warm woman's skin as soft as satin, rubbing against him everywhere, wanting to be touched, squeezed, taken.

She leaned up suddenly and put her face right next to

his, then her lips, moving slowly as a snake moves, up to its prey. Then she grabbed him and kissed him hard, probing her long, sinuous tongue into his lips, making his tongue strike back.

He took over her mouth and filled it as he felt his maleness want to take her, fill her, fill every part of her.

"Come on." She laughed, pulling back impulsively. "Let's have fun. Thats what I'm here for—to give you fun. And I think you're the kind of guy who knows how to have fun. Don't you, you cute thing?"

"Could be," Stone said stupidly, knowing he was grinning like a schoolboy in the throes of full desire. Between just killing a man and full-fledged sexual lust in the space of a few seconds, his head was spinning a little too fast, like that poor bastard in the roulette wheel. What a headache he must have.

"What's your name?" she asked, laughing in a girlish way, as if they were out on their first date. "Mine's Triste. Triste for sadness. Although I don't feel sad tonight." She smiled, pulling him into one of the elevators. They squeezed to the back between some gangsters, their whores for the night cradled under their arms like little red-faced dolls.

"I'm Staloni, Vito Staloni," he said, feeling as if he were under her hypnotic power, as if he would just follow her wherever she went and answer every question.

"Nice name," Triste said, taking her index finger and tracing it between his lips. "You have nice lips too. I'd like to feel them on my body." She ran her finger down along the inside of his thigh, just up to the heavy tool that hung inside, and then laughed again and danced away as the elevator doors opened to the main dance floor. She was a goddamned tease. But the best he'd ever seen. And Stone just stumbled after her like a stag in rutting season. Since the dawn of time all philosophers have known one basic truth: The cock is mightier than the brain.

Inside, the joint was jumping. The immense dance floor was filled with thugs and whores dancing out their hearts, jumping around without any sense of rhythm, flailing their hands and swinging their asses to the pounding beat of the music. On stage an all-female band, stark naked, was playing rousing dance numbers at an ear-shattering decibel level.

"Come on, let's dance," Triste said, pulling Stone's hand out toward the illuminated floor where they spun around and around. He made a few faltering steps trying to get into the proper mood when he looked down and almost lost his lunch. For cemented solid in clear plastic were bodies of men, lying side by side as if set out for burial. They lay horizontally just inches below the dance floor's transparent surface, staring up at the stomping hordes above. Dwarf's enemies or ready volunteers, the dozens of dead bodies that lay in perfectly even rows across the floor's length all appeared to be smiling as if wanting the living above to enjoy themselves, as if vicariously experiencing all the action from the grave.

Stone glanced up and saw the woman looking at him with amusement in her eyes.

"Aren't they wonderful?" She laughed with a high shriek that for a second rose above even the roar of the music and the crowd. "I just love Dwarf's sense of design." She laughed again and then closed her eyes and began grinding in fast circles at Stone. She was beautiful. There was just no two ways about it. He looked at her as the strobes and the blue and red and green light bulbs flickered on and off everywhere, putting the world in constant movement, a million shadows flickering off the walls and ceiling. She was beautiful, however the light struck her. He couldn't understand how she could be so cavalier about death, even be turned on by it when her face looked just the opposite: untouched. Of all the people in the place her eyes actually glowed, seemed alive, her lips always smiling, laughing, in motion. And yet there was a darkness in her, too, like the others. He was incredibly attracted to her and terrified of her at one and the same time.

They danced for nearly an hour, and Stone actually began to have a little bit of fun, even growing used to the dead faces that stared up at him, getting to like one in particular that he and Triste joked looked like Bob Hope. Then she was pressing up against him, closer and closer, until she seemed to be trying to mold her breasts, her thighs, against him. And he knew it was time. Time to leave. For a woman must be picked when ripe, so that desire will bring out the sweetest of her juices.

CHAPTER
Fifteen

SHE WAS on him. She was all over him. Her naked body writhing like an amphibious thing against his hard-muscled flesh. She seemed to want to feel the hardness of his body and squeezed at his arms again and again, hard. She pressed against him with her thighs just for a second, so her moist triangle of golden blond hair touched his swelling organ to feel it, and then pulled away again teasingly. She pushed him on his back and kissed his chest over and over with loud kisses, kneading the sides of his thighs—desperate, urgent squeezes. Then her mouth moved down to his stomach and then to the patch of coarse hair that began the forest around his manhood.

She moved her head down to the engorged tool and licked all around it, teasing. Then, lifting her mouth to the tip of the staff of flesh, she parted her wet lips, opened her mouth wide, and sank down onto the thing, letting out a hiss of air from between her nostrils, like a dolphin diving to submerge. She seemed to try to take the huge member all the way down but only got halfway before it completely filled her and she stopped, her throat clenching around the stiff spear in spasms of mad desire. As she grew accustomed to the length and thickness of him, she began moving up and down on the organ, taking it almost out and then as far down as she could, pushing farther at each attempt, until at last it filled her lips to the hilt, and Stone, lying on his back on the smooth and cool satin sheets, let out low animal noises as she took in all of him.

Suddenly her whole body seemed to go limp, and she began spasming, her upper body jerking madly as if in an erotic frenzy. She fell to the bed by his side, her face soft and open with Mona Lisa smile and wide, doelike eyes staring up at him from the darkness as her glowing field of spreading blond hair lay beneath her head and body like a cushion of fire.

"I need you," she groaned, her eyes hardly able to stay open as her lips vibrated with the tremors of unbridled animal desire. "Need you in me now. Please. Please!" Her words sounded urgent, and she spread her legs apart, lifting them at the same time so she was ready for him, completely open and ready for him to do with her what he wished.

Stone grabbed her strongly in each hand, knowing she wanted it that way, and pulled her hard toward him. He pushed his tongue deep into her throat and she swallowed that, too, as she had the now stiff organ below, which stood out like a flagpole of desire. He spread her legs and grabbed hold of the hard, burning mound of golden hair. She was wet and throbbing like a thing alive. Her lips parted readily for him the moment he touched them, the flushed, engorged lips spreading apart like petals opening for the sun. The red clitoris poked out from its soft sheath of flesh as if demanding his attention. Stone found her center and took the little ball of red-hot flesh between his fingers, rubbing it fast and hard.

She half screamed and half moaned with incredible pleasure, both pushing him off with her arms and at the same time grinding her hips toward him for more. He knew her. She could see that already. Knew just how to take her. Her body felt like it never had before. Felt like a fire was igniting in the very center of her stomach and spreading like lava down every nerve of her thighs and her breasts, spreading out like ripples, like tongues licking her from inside.

She let out a strange animallike meow as he suddenly stiffened two of his fingers and found her opening. He pushed in slowly but firmly, until he was embedded in her up to the knuckles. She seemed to fall back into a trance, her eyes closing and head rolling from side to side, the soft, angelic lips open and wet with saliva. He pushed hard and then rolled his fingers around inside her, opening up her swelling canals for the huge organ that was about to fill her. She grinded up against the hand, slowly at first, but then as she began spiraling around in circles against him, started going crazy again, jerking up hard against him, putting both hands around his fist as if trying to force the hand in farther, deeper, into her very core.

He pulled his fingers out and she groaned again, suddenly so empty inside, wanting him. He rose above her, leaning on one arm, and took the now huge staff of rigid flesh and placed the head inside the golden, wet triangle, searching for and then finding the red lips, which parted at his touch. He placed the organ just at the tip of her opening and then sank down into her, going deeper and deeper in one long thrust that seemed to fill her forever. She half screamed as the man thing took every part of her stomach and filled her with an explosive tension. She could hardly accept all of him, and she just lay there feeling the sensations of the blood-filled log that seemed to take the very core of her consciousness.

Then the ripples ran through her again, and she seemed to open up deep inside, so he slid even deeper into the mysterious pink softness of her deepest self. He set himself inside her and grabbed her around the buttocks, pulling her toward him. Then he started pumping. She slid up and down on the rod, wet as a river, the juices flowing out of her and covering his manhood and stomach. She pulled her legs back even farther, to make room for him, and then threw them up around his shoulders. He locked her backward, grabbing the legs beneath his arms, and then pushed forward even deeper.

It was as if he were mining her. The harder he pumped, the more she seemed to open. As if her body had lived just for this night, her breasts just for his hands to squeeze, her entrance just for him to find the full depth of. Then he suddenly seemed to go half mad himself and started banging into her like a jackhammer. He pumped with his strong thighs, his body just crashing into her again and again, shaking her very bones with passionate thrusts. She wrapped her arms around his back and pulled herself up even tighter against him, so her breasts were pressed flat against his hard chest and her thighs were spread wide-open, giving him absolute and complete entrance to her throbbing, wet treasures.

Suddenly she was on fire. The flames growing in every cell and sweeping up her veins until they were streams of fire and then rivers of burning sensation. She squeezed around him as he moved inside her so fast that it was as if they were both joined together, were one moving, moaning, crying-out flesh. She didn't know where she began any longer and he ended, just that he was all of her, taking all of her, deeper than she had ever been taken before. She screamed a loud, high-pitched scream as her entire back arched like a bridge. Her nails dug into his back, scratching deep gouges of flesh that oozed red.

Then she came, her back undulating like a snake, as she jerked wildly beneath his driving body. He could hardly hold on to her, as she seemed like a wild horse trying to escape and stay at the same instant. He plowed deeper and felt his own lava rising from his core. He pumped ever harder, straining, grinding in until he felt he would crush her very body to paste. Then he grew even larger, and she screamed beneath him as he lifted her up off the bed and stiffened as long and as hard as a steel beam within her. She felt as if her stomach would burst. Then he exploded a volcanic release of burning desire that set her body into another convulsive set of spasms and another moaning release.

At last they were both still and lay side by side, just their upper arms and thighs touching, making little sucking sounds as the sweat made them stick together. She lit a cigarette and smoked it, the glowing tip lighting them both with the softest of orange glows so she could see his strong young body, and he could see the curves of her melon breasts and the way her pubic hair seemed to glow with a fire that pulled him toward her, made him want to touch her.

And then he could hardly believe it. His heart not even still from the previous encounter, he already felt himself stiffening again. And knew from the way she was grabbing for him, demanding him, and moaning again in that woman-animal way that this was going to be one of the better nights of his life. And then there was only her and the way she melted beneath his body.

CHAPTER
Sixteen

WHEN HE awoke the next morning, she was gone. He had expected it, of course. But still he wanted her again. Smelled her perfume in the air lingering like a dream in almost solid form. At last he sighed, threw back the sheet, and walked to the balcony. The sun was low in the sky, so it was still early, about ten or eleven. From the wide window the view of the Utah landscape below, the first time he'd seen it in daylight, was truly breathtaking. It seemed as if he could see forever, mountains and valleys, rivers that drifted lazily south in meandering patterns. The sun was out for the first time in days, and the brilliant rays lit the snowcapped peaks of the mountain range, making the morning sparkle as if the whole world were capped with diamond hair and sparkling diamond eyes. He'd better not get too relaxed, Stone suddenly thought, seeing as how a number of people would most likely be trying to kill him on this fine, sunny day.

There was a knock at the door, and Stone started toward

153

his Uzi, which hung over a chair by the bed. A figure entered before he could reach his auto pistol or throw on a bit of clothing. He stood stark naked, frozen in mid-stride, wondering if the day's battle were to begin so early, before he'd even gotten his eyes half open. But it was just one of the service team, an old woman with disheveled hair and wild eyes carrying in his breakfast. By the blue pantsuit she wore, Stone thought, the kitchen help, too, must all be members of the illustrious ranks of the insane.

"Sorry," Stone said, blushing as he reached for his pants, hanging over the back of the armchair by the window, and quickly pulled them on, almost losing his balance in the process.

"That's okay," the ancient woman said, putting the tray filled with steaming, delicious odors down on a square table at the other side of the room. "I see naked men all the time. They come from the sky, at night sometimes, and through the wall. They all have penises. Penises, penises, they fly around me, they circle like vultures, their teeth opening and closing." She looked at Stone with an indescribable mix of madness and desire. "Do you think they'll hurt me—the flying penises?" she asked plaintively, like a little girl.

"No, I'm sure they won't," Stone answered as he pulled on his shirt, too, and tucked them into the jeans. And from the wrinkled, bag-eyed, gray-haired face and the huge stomach that made her look pregnant with triplets, Stone knew she had nothing to fear.

"Oh, goody, goody." She clapped her hands together and laughed, throwing her head back. But when the face came forward again, it wasn't smiling at all. "Will that be all, sir?" she asked, starting to retreat toward the partly opened front door.

"Let me ask you a question, if I could," Stone said a little hesitantly as he bent to pull on his boots. The woman stood waiting, emotionless, neither okaying nor denying Stone's request. "What—what is it like to be—be mad, to work for the Dwarf?" He knew he might be way out of line on the questions, but he had nothing to lose. All she could do was flip out and try to attack him with a butcher knife, an everyday occurrence for Martin Stone before he'd even had his coffee.

But she didn't go mad, though her face seemed to screw up in numerous contortions, as if the brain were working overtime on the question. "Well, I'm afraid I can't answer the first part of your question," the woman said, staring at Stone from across the room, her eyes burning like black coals in the cool morning air. "Because I'm not mad—you are—and all the penises in the Hotel. It is you who make the screams come—and the blood. Oh, the blood. The buckets of blood that I have cleaned in this hotel. The blood pouring down the stairs, on the walls, in the sheets. I didn't realize so much blood existed before. But now—" She seemed to grin for just a second, the narrow, crooked little teeth in her mouth all brown and mottled, like things about to tumble out. "Now I know my duty—to clean the blood and to stop the flying penises. And that is good. And it is simple. It is the way."

"What do you mean, 'the way'?" Stone asked, getting on his jacket as he loaded up his artillery, strapping it around waist and shoulder.

"The way—the way that the Dwarf teaches us. That one must know one's own abilities—and carry them out. He has been good to us. So good to us." The woman's eyes seemed to mist up, and she swept her bird's nest of hair back as if suddenly realizing she even existed. "Before the Dwarf helped me," the old, back-bent creature said, "there were only the faces of the dead and the blue fog. I had disappeared for many years. And when I woke, there was the Dwarf. And he gave me the way. He told me that cleaning blood was my destiny. And now I am free," the woman said, raising her arms to the ceiling. "Now I am a blood-cleaner—that is my calling."

"The others feel this way too?" Stone asked, fascinated by the mental control the twisted little man seemed to have over these wretched creatures.

"We are all grateful to Dwarf," the woman went on. "He has taken each of us from a pit of black fire where we knew neither ourselves nor each other—and put us back in the world again where we may at least live and breathe, and know that we are seeing another day. He has given us each a place and a function—and that is all that any living thing needs. He is the master, the maker, and the taker. He gives us the word of existence—and he takes it away, he shows us the way." Suddenly she dropped to her knees and began babbling incoherently, apparently praying to the Dwarf, asking for help against the attacking penises, which had begun their dive bomb attacks again. Suddenly she looked up, screamed, and ran from the room, batting at the air as if fending off invisible adversaries.

Stone shook his head slowly from side to side as he

walked over and closed, then locked, the door behind her.
He sat down and lifted the covers from the steaming food.
It was beautiful: eggs, bacon, French toast, orange juice,
even maple syrup, or what tasted close enough to it to do
the trick. How the Dwarf was able to get completely insane
men and women to serve him and actually be able to carry
out relatively complicated functions was amazing. The man
obviously had incredible powers of psychological control
and conditioning. If the war hadn't occurred—and Poet had
been more interested in helping mankind rather than per-
verting it and bringing it down to its lowest possible level,
he might have been a great man. Might have been able to
help the insane, the poor bastards lost in their eternal nightmares as the serving lady had been. At least she had a
function, Stone had to admit—a bloodcleaner. A vocation
that apparently brought her great satisfaction.

He walked out through the halls again, preferring to take
the rampways downstairs even though it was a long walk,
so he could have a total picture of the immense resort in
his mind. He had to start getting some kind of plan together,
but his head and thoughts seemed so fragmented from the
events of the previous day and the long night of super sex
that he could hardly think. He reached for thought but found
only mental mud.

There were more bodies from the previous night's festivities. And because it was still fairly early—for the Final
Resort, which didn't even really start swinging until midnight—they hadn't yet been taken away by the body crews.
A very young woman, naked, lying just outside a doorway
as if she'd been thrown there when . . . she broke. Then

another one on the seventeenth level, this one cut all over the place with what looked like a thousand little slices, with cigarette burns all over her breasts so they looked like cratered balls of meat. Stone suddenly wished he hadn't eaten breakfast and vowed not to eat another bite until he was out of this place.

On the fourteenth level he had to step through a wide puddle of blood with three bodies lying at its edges. Two of them were young boys, their faces contorted wide with the scream of super pain that Stone had seen on the head in the roulette wheel. They all seemed to go with that same look here. The Final Resort was not the best place to die—if dying was what you had in mind. He stepped as gingerly as he could through the puddle, a good eight feet in diameter, trying not to splash the red on his boots or pants. But he did. He headed down the next ramp, vowing to himself, somewhere in the deepest part of his soul, that he was going to take out the whole damned place. Not just rescue April but sink this rotten cesspool into the deepest pits of hell.

In the wide courtyard workmen were hooking together a wooden platform about twenty feet square and eight feet high. Stone sat on a bench outside one of the bars, now closed for restocking, broken glass, and body removal, and watched them work. They moved like ants, Dwarf's army of the insane, all wearing the same slit sunglasses, all working without talking to one another. Within an hour or so the place was packed with the pimps and slave buyers. At last a fat, bald-headed thing waddled to the front of the platform and addressed the crowd through a handheld microphone.

"Gooooood afternoon, ladies and gentlemen—if there are

any out there—pimps and madams, whoremasters and slave buyers." The fat-faced piece of lard had one of those deep, jocular, nonstop voices that radio announcers of prewar days had used. Only the products had changed. "Todaaay we have a large assortment of quality merchandise," the fat face spoke, its lips looking like they had been doing too much sucking of young flesh as they were thick, puffed out, like swollen tumorous worms. "None of those high-rad, low-quality girls that some of the auction houses have been trying to pass off as usable product. No siree bob." The announcer slapped his huge stomach, and it jiggled wildly inside his togalike outfit, like the egg of a dinosaur trying to hatch. "Like me—what you see is what you get."

The crowd of unshaven pimps and whore buyers laughed and applauded lightly. The guy put on a good show. You had to hand him that. Even if he had one of the ugliest faces in this whole part of the country.

"These girls are all meat of the highest quality—rad tested and documented, certified syphilis-, gonorrhea- and AIDS-free. And you get the documentation to go with it," the announcer said, holding up a bunch of papers with official-looking red seals on them. "So let's get the show on the road," the auctioneer said, wiping his bald, shiny head with a handkerchief, as it was already starting to sweat from the noon sun. "We got a long and hot afternoon ahead of us." He clapped his hands sharply, and two assistants led a bunch of women up some stairs from the back of the platform to the side, where they stood in a mute line, hands cuffed together in front of them, steel collars around their necks. Each collar was attached to the one behind it by means of a long chain that one of the assistants unlocked and slid down the line, freeing them from the chain gang.

The fat man clapped again, and an assistant—a young, strikingly effeminate boy with lipstick and rouge on his face, dressed in a similar toga as the auctioneer's only brown— grabbed the first woman on the line and dragged her over until she was at the very front of the platform on a small raised wheel of wood about a yard wide.

"Now, I ask you, do we give you shoddy merchandise?" The fat man laughed, walking the few steps over to the young beauty, breathing hard at each step, as he had so much to carry. "Look at this young lovely, will you?" He lifted her long red hair, which flowed like a river of fire covering her face, and flipped it back over her shoulders. The crowd gasped. She was like an angel. A little precious diamond whose perfect purity would give them that much more delight in soiling. For they would use her beauty, would suck it from her like a wasp sucks the innards of a butterfly, leaving only a shriveled, empty husk behind that rolls away in the lightest breeze, as it is no longer with form or substance.

So they looked at her breathtaking pink nubility with erections and red faces, each imagining already what they would do with the perfect piece of meat if they could just get their hands on it.

"She's perfect in every way," the fat man said, suddenly unfastening the front of her short, coarsely woven garment. Her pear-sized white breasts popped out and stood straight, as if staring defiantly at the crowd, the nipples like little jewels of pink at the very tips. Lips were licked, teeth grinded together throughout the courtyard. The auctioneer ran his hands up and down her flesh, squeezing the young breasts hard in each hand and then letting them go.

"See how they bounce back? Firm, firm as young veal." He reached down and stroked her flanks, golden-haired flesh of perfect, curved beauty, and then sank to one knee. "She even makes *me* want to crawl before her." The auctioneer laughed. He put one greasy hand up against her red triangle of hair and spread the lips apart, placing a thick finger up to her entrance.

"And," he mock-whispered into the microphone, though all of the thousand people in the courtyard could hear every word. "Believe it or not, she's a virgin. Look, I can't even get my finger in there." He pretended to push hard and then rose to his feet, stumbling and again gasping for air for a few seconds.

"And that's official too. Documented virgin—not one of those reprocessed, hand-sewn jobs. Why, you can't even buy these anymore." The fat face laughed again, walking slowly back and forth on the stage, trying to get them all going, trying to whip the crowd into the kind of frenzy that would really make the money flow. Would make them like piranha, attacking whatever he presented to them in blind lust and need. "A real, one-hundred-percent low-rad virgin."

The girl of such perfect beauty couldn't have been more than sixteen. She stood with her hands cuffed in front of her, trying to cover her most private parts, and stared blankly down at the wooden planks beneath her feet, ashamed, knowing that whichever of the faces that devoured her from below ended up getting her—she was doomed. She only prayed that she could find a way to end it all before the torture became too unbearable.

"Now, I'm not even going to set a low bid on this precious jewel," the auctioneer yelled into the mike, so his lewd voice echoed up through the myriad levels of the resort. "'Cause I can't even imagine what it would be. So you tell me—what is this piece of perfect edible flesh worth to you?"

"A thousand dollars," a particularly ugly specimen near the platform yelled out. Stone caught a glimpse of the thing's face. It had teeth and a nose, but only the fact that it was wearing a long black bearskin coat and could talk offered any proof that it was human. The face looked more like a caveman's, with low-ridged brow and hair covering every part of it, even the forehead. Stone shuddered. The idea of that young girl ending up with something like that. He wondered how many of them he could get if he just opened up right where he was standing with both weapons. Then he banished the absurd idea down into the lower regions of his brain where it spat and kicked for quite a while.

"One thousand, that's a nice round number," the fat-faced auctioneer said into the mike. "But I think we can get more, a lot more."

"Two thousand," another voice screamed, a woman this time. Stone looked through the crowd and saw her, a heavily pancake-layered madam with huge bosom and perfumes and powder coating her like flour on a cake. She knew what a true virgin that looked like that would get in the right circles. The bidding went back and forth for nearly two minutes, several others joining in. But at last it was down to the madam and the caveman, and the bid had risen to ten thousand dollars, an extraordinary price for any slave or whore.

"Eleven thousand," the madam said, fanning her face with a Japanese brocaded fan.

"Eleven thousand," the auctioneer yelled out, turning to the caveman. "Do I hear twelve? Twelve?" But the fur-faced bidder had had enough. He was just a mountain thief, how the hell could he compete with these big-time operators from the cities? He spat and waved his hand, signaling that he'd had enough.

"Sold to the attractive woman in blue," the auctioneer said. "You can pick her up in the side holding pen after the auction. All payments at that time—in cash or adjudged equivalent. No checks, credit cards, or live animals," the fat face scolded the audience. Again they laughed; this guy was a real punch in the face. Stone was glad at least for the first girl that the madam had gotten her. Whatever her fate, it couldn't be worse than ending up with fur-lips.

The auctioneer brought out the next two, stripped their gowns down, and started his rap. "Twins from Dakota— not yet seventeen and still semi-virgins. No cuts, bruises, or open wounds—that you can see," he added, laughing slyly into the mike. "Now shall we begin the bidding at . . ."

The auction went on for hours as Stone stared in amazement at the proceedings. Young girls, middle-aged women, men, boys, even Siamese twins were all brought out and paraded around. Their breasts and buttocks were squeezed, their mouths opened and teeth shown. Then they were bid on and bought by the crowd. Brought singly, in small groups, and in lots as big as two dozen, which afforded the buyer something of a discount.

Martin Stone had never felt so helpless in his life. So many lives, so much pain and death—and he couldn't do a thing about it. Then he saw something that made him feel a lot worse than that—he saw April being paraded up onto the platform and led to the front so the crowd could get a good look at the glistening young treasure that just happened to be his sister.

He couldn't even look as the fat hands exposed her body, turned her, and prodded her. Then the bidding started. A group of men on the far side of the platform, out of Stone's sight, wanted her, and the price was quickly over a thousand. Stone gulped, knowing that to even draw the slightest bit of attention to himself at this stage of the game could be his death sentence, and then yelled out.

"Twelve hundred. I bid twelve!" The auctioneer saw Stone's raised arm and took the bid.

"Twelve, come now, someone must bid thirteen for such a fine, narrow-waisted specimen," the fat lips exhorted the crowd.

"Thirteen," a man yelled out. Again Stone couldn't see.

"Fourteen," he shouted at the auctioneer, who looked back, pointing a fat finger at him. Stone had no idea where he was going to get all the money, but he'd worry about that later. Once he was even near April, maybe he would just make his move. The sooner they were both out of the place, the better. The very air of the courtyard made his skin crawl, as if it were infested with disease, madness, and the unseen mist of the blood of its numerous victims.

"Fifteen!" the voice boomed out from about twenty yards away.

"Christ, sixteen," Stone screamed back, standing up now, forgetting he was supposed to be at low visibility today. He could hardly stand it anymore—bidding for his own sister with scum who didn't even deserve to be walking on the face of the earth. The bidding went back and forth for nearly a minute, at last rising to a peak of thirty-five hundred, Stone's last bid. The auctioneer pointed to the other voice.

"Going once, twice, three times, sold to the gentlemen in the pink suit. Please collect your prize, you lucky fellow, behind the platform. Payment in cash only." Stone walked through the crowd, feeling again for his weapons. He had no idea quite what he was going to do now, but he'd been playing it all by ear since the moment he left the shelter— why stop now? He came around the back where wooden cages had been set up in which scores of softly whimpering girls still waited for their turn to be marketed, like so many pigs in their pen. Stone walked up to a man sitting down at a table.

"I just bought number 271," Stone said, referring to the number that had been written on her back.

"Oh, yes," the bearded face said, looking up. "We've been expecting you."

"What the hell do you mean expect—" Stone started to say, stepping back as he sensed trouble. But he never got to finish the question. A steel net suddenly dropped down from above, landing on his head and shoulders and knocking him instantly to the ground. Guards jumped from every shadow, submachine guns in hand, and walked toward Stone, who struggled on the ground like a fish out of water. He tried to swing the Uzi around, but a foot suddenly slammed down from above, hitting him in the hand, breaking two fingers. He pulled back, wincing in pain.

"Ah, Mr. Stone, I'm so, so glad you could be here in time for Christmas festivities," a high-pitched voice squealed from the side. Stone turned his head. It was the Dwarf, sitting in his motorized wheelchair. Stone had almost forgotten just how repulsive the armless and legless stump of pasty flesh was, but one look quickly reminded him. The thing hardly seemed human, more like something that should have been flushed down the toilet the moment it was born instead of being allowed to grow, to fester like the living virus that it was. The egg-shaped thing sat there with sunglasses over his ovular, misshapen face, stabbing with his uneven stumps at the buttons that controlled the wheelchair's movements and systems control. It sped around the perimeter of the net, addressing Stone from a constant state of motion, so the Dwarf's face kept spinning around him.

"Really, you were so predictable—it's quite pitiful," the lump of flesh spoke from the chair, the thin lips hardly moving. The thing looked more like a dummy than a real person, like something not born of flesh but of a sterner, crueler substance. "The compassionate—or those who fancy themselves such things, those who care about something—they are the easiest to capture and destroy," the Dwarf went on, gloating over the capture of the man he had wanted most to find and destroy. "All you have to do is set a trap for them. Take what they care about and they will come searching for it. They have to. You and your kind—you are like dogs after bone, or ants scenting sugar." The guards began rolling the nets forward from every side, so Stone was contained in a tighter and tighter steel-mesh cage.

"What is the sound of death, Stone?" the squirming mound of flesh asked, its thin lips stretching back in a skeletal grin. The dwarf, as always, gave the answer to the Zen koan of violence after a few seconds. "It is the sound that only the earless can hear, and the voiceless can speak, Martin Stone. The language of the grave."

Then the heavy boots of the guards were slamming into Stone as if they were trying to crack him into splinters. He tried to shield himself, but it was impossible, they were everywhere. Then the endless rain of blows seemed to turn into pure sound, and all Stone could hear were thunderous crashes, and he didn't know if they were coming from outside or inside his own body. And he couldn't help but wonder, as he spun off into a very dark place, if it was the music of the grave he was hearing, and the boots that smashed him into little pieces, the feet of the dancing dead.

CHAPTER
Seventeen

RATS! RATS all around him, floating in the water, swimming around his face. In the darkness he could see the pointed noses coming straight toward him, like sleek-furred alligators, the long jaws opening, fangs flashing ivory as the claws paddled furiously through the dark waters, creating furrows of bubbling foam. Were there rats in hell? Stone wondered absurdly, his last conscious thought having been of the Dwarf's send-off. But the few straggly rays of light that razored in between the bars of a window on a far wall told him he was still of this earth. In a cell with thick concrete walls and, filling the whole bottom, a pool of water in which he was floating.

A loud splashing sound caught his eye just to the side, and Stone turned his still dazed head to see a rat the size of a barracuda bearing down on him, its eyes blazing like little black coals in the near darkness of the cell. Its teeth, spread wide apart, hissed out a sound of animal hunger. Stone pulled at his arms to strike the thing away, but he was tied. Tied to a pole. And chest-deep in thick, foul-smelling water, sitting on something, a chair of some kind, so he didn't sink while unconscious.

"Fucking shit!" Stone yelled out as he discovered he had no functioning arms or hands. The scream echoed wetly off the algae- and slime-covered walls around him, and a few things splashed off in the distance. The thing was almost upon him now, the fangs in the front of the wedge-shaped face, a good inch long, enough to sink in and take a pretty good bite. In desperation Stone ripped up his right leg with all his might and it moved. The booted foot came shooting up from the depths and broke the surface, catching the madly stroking vermin dead center of its stomach. The black waterlogged shape, squealing wildly, shot up into the air in the spray of water and disappeared, clawing at the air several yards away.

"This is great," Stone yelled out. "What kind of accommodations are these? I'll never bring my business here again, I'll tell you that." He shut up as the yelling made his head start to split with an electric headache. He could feel that his skull was covered with blood and bumps. The bastards had done the best they could to strike brain tissue. And since he felt pretty dizzy, for all Stone knew, he was working on half empty.

Not really wanting to, he looked around the cell as his eyes slowly adjusted to what little bit of light was coming in. He was in a cinder-block cell about thirty feet square. The pool of water seemed to be about four feet high, and he couldn't tell at first, but after a minute he decided that the level was rising slowly up. The rat population was not closing in for the kill after his kicking off of the last visitor, but they sure as hell were eyeing him with plenty of interest. The oil-slicked shapes swam back and forth just yards away, their red eyes examining him carefully, searching for weakness, for the scent of blood. They seemed to be everywhere, the pool of brackish black filled with slapping, biting, splashing, and breathing sounds, like a zoo in hell. He was the biggest piece of food any of the rodents had ever seen. Even the oldest, an immense two-foot-long black-furred one that sat on a ledge in pitch blackness directly across from Stone and just watched—and waited. It knew about death. Knew there was all the time in the world for the thing to die, to stop its useless flailings. Then it would feed. Would move in. It would take its place at the top of the hierarchy of the foul, scum-encrusted pool of black swamp water, in which the meat eaters dwelled. Would take its rightful first pickings. So it stared at Stone's mouth. Because that's what it wanted. The lips, and the tongue that it could see moving inside when the creature emitted sounds of pain. The tongue. The one-eared rat stared at Stone's mouth with its own form of lust, visualizing in short and barely formed vermin daydreams how good it would taste to bite into it.

There were more than just rats inhabiting the place Stone was pleased to discover as he turned his head to the side and saw a long, slithering shape crawling down the metal pipe to which his hands were tied. Stone moved his face closer, trying to see, in the few dabs of light that reached him, what it was. And he wished he hadn't. A millipede, its thousand legs whipping away beneath it as it beelined straight for Stone, with dinner the thought clearly foremost in its mind. It was a huge, ugly thing with long, curved pincers snapping open and closed as it undulated down the pipe. Aside from not wanting a piece of his hand to end up in the thing's jaws, Stone knew they could be poisonous. That was all he needed, on top of everything, some nice millipede venom flowing through his veins.

He struggled furiously as the thing slithered closer, but the hands were clasped around the pipe with metal handcuffs that didn't appear about to come apart.

"Fuck off, little squirming scumbag," Stone yelled at the thing, his mouth only about a foot away from it. But if it heard the threatening words, it didn't show it, just kept on slithering closer, the pincers now wide apart like a pair of scissors about to snap shut. Stone pulled back as far as he could, his arms stretched out to their fullest, and again kicked up with his leg. The boot and pants were sogging with the slime water and made the leg feel as heavy as a log. But somehow it launched itself up out of the surface, creating a huge splash that splattered over Stone's mouth and eyes, leaving an indescribably terrible taste in his mouth. The foot shot up toward the pipe and made contact just inches away from the millipede. It scampered out of the way—and just kept coming on.

"Fucking little bastard, die!" Stone screamed, whipping the foot up again the moment it came down into the water. This time the aim was better, and the steel-tipped toe of the heavy boot slammed right into the overlegged thing's back, squashing half of it into green paste against the pipe. The two other parts fell away to each side and hit the black water with little splashes, sinking down, attracting other things that swam toward the still struggling parts, drawn by their motion. Stone's leg flopped back down into the water, and the waves sent out by the exertions headed out across the black pool, sending a chorus of protests up from the hell-hole's denizens, which slithered and hissed, spat, and rearranged themselves as the water splashed over them.

As his eyes adjusted even further, Stone saw that the walls of the place were completely covered with bugs, hanging on to every square inch of it—centipedes, millipedes, roaches of gargantuan proportions, bedbugs and silverfish, beetles, and writhing larvae that rolled over anything near them, trying to catch them in their sticky mass and absorb them. Immense spiderwebs draped down from the ceiling and the corners were filled with the plating and exoskeletons of past victims. Even through the darkness Stone could see the owner of one web, nearly a foot long and hairy, with long, jointed legs, standing in the darkest part of the darkness, waiting for its food to come to it.

"I told the snake man this was my kind of place," Stone whispered to himself in the darkness, talking so he wouldn't go mad, wouldn't lose his sanity in the foul slime of the place. For once he went over the edge in *this* blackness, he would never return. "Why, I've got my own private basement condo—wet tub and all." Stone giggled, feeling his rational mind starting to edge toward the abyss again. "And lots of friends, yes, you meet so many nice—things—at Club Dead," Stone whispered now as the shadows began circling closer again in the oily black water.

The standoff continued for hours. Each time one of the shadows came too close, whatever it was, Stone would scream and kick out with his leg, driving it off. But they knew he was weakening and soon would not have the strength to strike out at them. The inhabitants of the foul, watery world all moved in around him, coming from out of every little crevice, every filthy hole and crack, to get their share. There would be plenty for everybody.

Stone knew the waters were rising. Not rapidly but every hour, or as far as he could gauge an hour to be, the black sludge rose about an inch. When he had awoken from unconsciousness, the swamp had reached mid-chest—now it was approaching the base of his throat. And then—

He thought it was going to be the rats that would give him the most trouble, as they were the biggest, but when the first real attack came, it was from the roaches. Seeing the water covering everything but his head, and not seeing any weapons the big creature could use on them, the dark legions from the ceiling began getting whipped up into a feeding frenzy. Then, as if at a single command, they started forward, wave after wave of brown shell and probing antennae, heading down the wall nearest to Stone, about six feet away in the water. These weren't your dear-there's-a-bug-in-the-garbage type of insects; these were monsters, the average-sized ones as big as Stone's fingers and the really big ones, black with immense antennae nearly a half foot long, were as large as mice or small rats. And they were hungry too. They hadn't launched this big an invasion since an alley cat had somehow made its way in the year before and they'd been among the first of the cell's meat eaters to close in. Stone could hear their high-pitched squealing, almost inaudible shrieks of hunger, their thousands of legs and mandibles scraping against one another so a rushing sound, almost of wheat blowing in the wind, seemed to fill the cell.

Stone was sure the water would stop them, but when the advance ranks reached the black liquid, they just kept going. The lead roaches stepped forward right into the water and then stopped, letting the ones behind them walk over their backs and into the liquid. Thus sacrificing themselves, even drowning but being held in place by the mandibles clamped around their front and hind legs, the army of whispering bugs began building a bridge out of their own bodies, a bridge that was aimed straight at Stone and was being built at the rate of about three inches a minute.

"Good God." He half groaned as he saw the blanket of brown spreading across the foul water, an armada of chomping little jaws and teeth. He didn't think he could take much more of this. The water was up to his chin, even standing, as he had been for hours. He strained to move higher, but the cuffs had snagged around a second beam welded to the pipe and wouldn't go an inch higher. He tried to whip his leg up and at least create a disturbance in the water. But the leg couldn't even reach the surface now, just rising to within about a foot of the air and then sinking back down.

Stone screamed out as the fleet of brown closed in, now just inches away.

"Fuck off, get the fuck off me, fuck off, fuck off." It was primitive language for the most primitive of situations. If only he could kill himself, Stone suddenly wished with all his heart. A gun, even a knife. But there was nothing, no way. He was going to be eaten micro-bite at a time by filth-coated roaches. He began swinging his head wildly around in the water, trying to set up little waves that would dislodge the roach bridge, send it floating off. But though the entire structure, consisting now of thousands of already lifeless bodies, their living comrades advancing en masse over their backs, shook and wriggled up and down like the surface of a water bed, nothing dislodged, not a single brown nightmare floating off.

The very first landing party was just inches off now, and one of them leapt suddenly forward, landing on Stone's nose. It grabbed hold of a nostril and immediately turned to head for his eye, which for some reason it had its mandibles set on. Stone shook like a wild man now, whipping his entire skull from side to side like a mace on the end of his spinal cord. The roach went flying, and the nearest little extension of brown bridge broke off and sank. He spun his head around, fighting off everything as they tried to land, tried to establish their beachheads. He shook off the roaches, the spiders, the slugs, and the waterbugs, fought back the snakes and the rats. Martin Stone fought off every goddamned thing that was trying to get to know him better, and as a few landed on his mouth—for better or worse—ate those that were trying to eat him.

CHAPTER
Eighteen

H E SWORE he heard Christmas music, the strains of "Jingle Bells," and voices laughing. How could rats laugh, or roaches play accordion? Stone wondered as he flailed out at the air in front of him. They were almost on him, those black, pointed faces, those mandibles, those jaws. He punched and punched and heard laughter again. And suddenly he realized he was using his hands. He opened his eyes and saw that he was alive and was surrounded by human, rather than oily, black-pelted, vermin.

"Stone, Stone." A voice was laughing at his side. "You are so amusing, it's really quite wonderful." Stone turned and saw that pasty face, flesh the consistency of rotting dough, staring back at him. The dwarf wasn't wearing his shades now, and the pinhole eyes that hid behind folds of enflamed eyelid looked dark, like black holes that led nowhere. The egg-shaped thing tried to clap in pleasure but was only able to swing its stumps in the air, flapping like an amputated penguin as it laughed that hideous, cackling dummy sound again, which made Stone wish he was back with the bugs and his other pals in the black swamp.

"But, really, did you think I would let you die, Mr. Stone? When I went to so much trouble to lure you here—and then capture you? No—no, you are to be my guest for the Christmas Pageant. The festivities that make life worth living, that reunite friends in closer harmony. Why, look around you, only the most elect group of super-sophisticated individuals are permitted to attend my private celebration." Stone looked around and saw that he was in a large banquet hall with four long tables running down each side of the room, covered with silk cloths and plates of exquisite china. If the hundred or so guests who sat around them were the Dwarf's definition of polished guests, Stone couldn't tell the difference between them and rest of the pea-brained sludge who were staying at the resort, except perhaps that their eyes seemed at least to see what was happening around them.

He looked down and saw that he was chained to the chair. His arms had movement but only enough to reach for food on the table and eat it. He was Dwarf's guest for the duration.

"Tell me, Mr. Stone, what is the sound of a rat biting?" the Dwarf asked, leaning back in his wheelchair, prepared to enjoy the evening to its utmost. Large-breasted blond women hovered all around him, giving him sips of liquor and wine from crystal goblets they held out in front of his lips. The man didn't need arms and legs—he had a city of slaves who would attend to his every function.

"Your teeth coming down on that glass," Stone spat back as he settled into the chair and reached for a glass of rose-colored wine that sat in front of him. If they were going to poison him—so much the better. Anything quicker than twelve hours was fine with him. Stone leaned back and drained the glass and felt the pleasant fire of the alcohol sweep through his gullet. At least he'd die on a full stomach.

"Not bad, Stone," the Dwarf shrieked out. "Only not true, of course. I am not a rat. I am not a man. What am I, Stone? Do you know?"

"You're an evil, putrid, ugly piece of protoplasmic rot that should be heaved down the nearest sewer, Dwarf," Stone said, leaning forward and refilling his glass.

"Yes, no doubt all true," the Dwarf said. "But that's just the physical dimension. There's something more. Something deeper. Do you know, Stone? Know what I am, really am?"

"If you mean do I know the exact diagnosis of your mental condition—schizophrenic, paranoid schizophrenic, or just plain psychopathic—no, I don't, Dwarf," Stone said, leaning back and draining another small goblet of the rippling ruby wine.

"I'm the opposite, Stone. The opposite of all that you are, the opposite of all that you believe and hope for. I am the shadow to the light of your soul, Stone. And though I carry out my darkness against all men, I think your destiny and mine cross. . . . Pure antithetical elements face-to-face— your matter to my antimatter. But tonight I win. Tonight the darkness conquers again, Stone. The war was just the start. Now the fire of civilization flickers down to small little flames—and I prepare to blow it out. Then darkness will fall, Stone, total darkness. Will fall over America and then the entire world. And I shall oversee it, its implementation, its very battle against the light, until all the flames are extinguished and the earth is as cold and barren as the moon."

"Why?" Stone asked, feeling sickened by the speech. He hadn't realized the twisted little egg-thing even had a coherent philosophy. "Why are you so poisoned, so eager to destroy the human race?" Stone asked, taking another drink and then pouring yet another. He felt like getting drunk tonight, roaring drunk.

"Why? Why?" the Dwarf asked, shaking its arm stumps around in the air like little dark knobs, laughing as it shook. It was in fine humor tonight. "Just look at me. I am the most twisted of all. And I represent all that is twisted. You normal and sane and straight people created this world— this hell of atomic rains and slow elimination of the species by radiation poisoning. You created me out of the chemicals that my mother took that made me this way. But from my birth I knew, Stone, knew that I was more than myself, that I was to take the cares of all the ugly, diseased, and twisted people upon my shoulders. And I was going to carry out their wishes. I am the chosen one, Stone. The ugliest of the ugly. And I am here to take us all into hell, where we belong. For I am the death desire itself of the human species. And I exist only to carry out that most secret of man's desires, his deepest, most unspoken wish—for total destruction. Total and complete decimation of every insect, every blade of grass on the face of the earth. This is my destiny." With that moving speech given, the egg man half fell back in the wheelchair as a female hand reached around and wiped sweat from his brow with a cool, ice-filled cloth.

"Sounds like a great idea," Stone said, swigging down his fourth glass of wine in five minutes. "The destruction of the earth is an idea that's long overdue. Now, when's dinner? I thought this was going to be a whole big shindig or something," Stone yelled, burping. "Swimming the breaststroke for all those hours built up quite an appetite."

"Indeed, indeed," the Dwarf said, sitting up straight and pushing a button on the panel built into the side of the electric wheelchair. "Let the Christmas feast begin," the Dwarf said, laughing again and clapping its stumps at empty air. Servants came in from everywhere, stepping from behind high curtains. On their shoulders they carried immense trays that were quickly set down on the tables. Roasts, potatoes, creamed onions, puddings, pies, stuffings, cranberry sauces. All the traditional Christmas fare, and it smelled delicious, though strongly spiced.

"Christmas demands more in the way of feasting," the Dwarf said, addressing the tables full of thugs, murderers, and mutilators who listened with happy holiday spirits, downing gallons of hard liquor so that they were all already glassy-eyed and as stupid as cows. "Christmas demands sweeter flavors, sweeter tastes. Do you know what the sweetest meat is, Stone?" the Dwarf asked, twisting around in his wheelchair so that he addressed Stone, who sat opposite him and about six feet away.

"Can't say for sure, slime, but I would think pork with

applesauce," Stone said, reaching forward to fill his plate with the delicious offerings.

"No, there's one meat sweeter than all the rest Stone— the sweetpig—man. The flavor that once tasted, you never forget." Stone fought the urge to bring up everything he had chewed down in the last week and put his plate down in front of him in the middle of filling it to overflow. He looked closely. The meat—it was unusually white and fatty. And the potatoes—he gagged as he stared a little deeper into the sauce—were eyes, human eyeballs, deveined and pupiled, white orbs of gelatinous flesh in a thick cream sauce.

"Good God," Stone whispered to himself as he backed away in horror from the table, trying to get as much distance between his body and the "food" as he could. He pulled back in the chair as if trying to go through it. Suddenly the odors that had filled his stomach with ravenous growls smelled putrid and sickly sweet.

One of the female attendants cut Dwarf's portion and began feeding him bite-sized cubes, which he gobbled down like a white, wingless bird, a slug of sickness and hunger. Stone could hardly believe his eyes as the others who sat at the tables also began cutting and lifting portions of the human holiday gourmet platters to their mouths and chewing with gusto. Compliments to the chef were yelled out from numerous chairs.

"Not hungry, Stone?" Dwarf laughed again, from across the table filled with slices of human leg and breast, slabs of tongue ready to be piled on rye bread with just a dab of mustard. "How about some liquid refreshment, then?" The pasty egg man poked his right stump at a button, and two of the waiters walked in, pushing a large table on wheels. Atop the table was a woman, about eighteen, naked as the day she was born and strapped down with numerous leather thongs to the wooden top. And Stone again felt his stomach rise up like Vesuvius ready to go at a moment's notice. For inserted in her still pumping throat was a spigot, dug right into the jugular vein. He caught her eyes as she came by, and Stone could see that they were wide and moving madly from side to side in terror. Her body must have been paralyzed with a muscle drug, but her mind knew everything that was happening.

"The Masai of East Africa drink cow blood," Dwarf said as one of his attendants reached forward and turned the spigot just below the white throat. "They shoot an arrow into the living creature's throat and collect its blood in a gourd—and drink it on the spot. They have the right idea," the Dwarf said as the blood of the girl poured into a crystal decanter just a foot away from his face. "But human blood is even better. We do, after all, share the same common minerals and elements. Human blood is nature's most perfect food—for another human." The Dwarf laughed again, that hideous falsetto cackle, so he almost sounded like a little girl screaming, and the blonde lifted the glass of hot blood to his pale lips. The Dwarf drank long and deep, tilting his head back until the glass was drained. "Ah, so good, so good." He waved his stumps at the men who were handling the human barrel of blood. "Take her to everybody, you idiots. While the blood is still hot—before she dies. All the vitamins are lost once the blood starts turning cold."

The Dwarf again pushed a button, his lips now bright red from the blood cola. A whole crew of the Mad, wearing their distinctive blue ski jumpsuits came in carrying an immense plastic bubble a good twenty feet in diameter. They set it down right in the center of the room between the tables, so that everyone was afforded an equally good view.

"Now, I thought that we should allow our animal friends to partake of the Christmas spirit as well," the Dwarf said, addressing the drunken, drug-dazed diners, many of whom had already passed out, chunks of human meat hanging from their parted lips. "So I have picked a token representative from the animal world whom we shall allow to feast alongside us. Man and animal feeding in harmony together. Ah, what a beautiful thought."

Stone turned his head as he saw one side of the plastic bubble open and a young girl thrown inside, again naked, the way Dwarf liked them. She ran this way and that, bouncing off the curved, clear sides of the inch-thick Plexiglas wall, totally impervious to her frantic fists. She saw the faces, the empty, ugly faces staring at her from everywhere. It was like a bad dream—only it was real. All too real. For as she watched, the plastic container was again opened and she almost swooned and fell to the floor as she saw the five men on the other side feed their load inside. A snake. An immense snake, bigger than any Stone had ever seen. It must have been a good twenty-five feet long and bigger around than his chest. The thing was still curled in a big ball but quickly untangled itself and lifted its head slowly up like a periscope, which turned, whipping a long red tongue in and out quicker than the eye could see, sampling the air for scent.

Then it picked the girl out with its eyes and stopped moving, locking onto her like a tracking dish onto a missile. The girl screamed and screamed again. She ran frantically, but there was nowhere to go, and her naked feet just slipped off the curved plastic, like a hamster scampering around a wheel. The crowd woke up out of their stupors and began laughing and whistling their approval of the Dwarf's evening entertainment.

The snake's head came down, and it gathered itself together as the girl pulled as far as she could to the far side. Then it launched itself forward, moving with incredible speed for something that must have weighed several tons. The jaws snapped open and then closed right around the head of the screaming woman and snapped shut, the fangs digging deep into her neck so it almost appeared they went through to the other side. Yet the girl was still alive, her hands pressing against the sides of the yard-long jaws, as if trying to rip herself free. Her legs and feet moved frantically around the floor, running like a chicken with its head cut off.

Dwarf slapped his stumps back against the leather, swinging his whole wretched body from side to side, so the armless limbs whacked into the back of the chair with loud sounds. "It's even better than I had hoped," he said with a laugh. "Isn't it spectacular, Stone?" the Dwarf asked, looking over, so wanting his guest to like the night's entertainment. But Stone was speechless, his face white as the silk tablecloths those around him were eating their sweetmeats from.

The girl kept struggling, her young body just jumping all over the place like a fish out of water but not out of fighting spirit. But the snake knew, even if the female didn't, that it was all over. It settled down, stretching its body out along the bubble so it fit almost all the way around. Then it just let the muscles in its throat start pulling her down, inexorably down. It opened the mouth wide, to give space for the swallowing process, dislocating the back of the jaw. And down she went. Slowly, an inch at a time. The throat of the immense snake would vibrate, and then rough, teeth-like cilia that lined it internally would undulate, pulling the prey in, toward the waiting digestive fluids.

First her head, then shoulders, disappeared within. Within minutes the mouth was up to her waist, and the girl's arms could still be seen poking against the inside of the snake, as if she were trying to punch her way out. Then it opened even wider, seemed to gulp, and took her in to the knees— and still the legs kept pumping, so that all who watched knew she was still alive. And wondered what it would be like to be inside that scaly thing, down in the center of its acidic throat, in the darkness, feeling yourself being dissolved away, so slowly, and knowing, knowing every second, just what was happening. Even the hardest of the hard rocks who sat around the master dining room felt shudders run up and down their drug-saturated systems.

At last the snake had enveloped her all the way down to her ankles, and with a final shudder it gulped hard and she was completely inside. The huge serpent closed its eyes, ready to sleep in happy dreams while it digested its holiday bird.

"Oh, the evening is everything I'd hoped it would be." The Dwarf laughed, clapping his arm stumps in the air. "Everything is perfect, just perfect."

CHAPTER
Nineteen

BUT IF Stone thought things were bad, they suddenly got a thousand times worse. For once the Dwarf had the snake removed, so full of the occasionally still kicking human prey that it could hardly move and lay draped over the half dozen attendants' arms like a huge dangling fire hose, it was his turn. Stone was bodily removed from his chair and taken to the plastic cage himself where he was heaved unceremoniously inside. He withdrew to the far side, stepping through his cuffed arms so his hands and arms were at least in front of him. And his legs were free—he could kick. Though what good kicking against a snake was going to do, he couldn't imagine.

But within seconds it became clear that he wasn't going to be facing the snake but a human adversary—or something that had once been human. Stone stared at the figure that walked around the bubble, staring in at him contemptuously. Its face was distorted slightly by the curve of the plastic but not enough so that Stone didn't know for sure that it was just about the scariest fucking thing he'd ever seen—seven feet tall, with shoulders as wide as one of the banquet tables and muscles that would have made Arnold Schwarzenegger turn in his bodybuilding badge. But it wasn't the strength or size of the thing that made Stone wish he could crawl under a blanket with some milk and cookies—it was the face. For the thing had no face. It had been burned terribly by radiation years before; the gamma radiation that had been released by the sudden detonation of a nearby hydrogen bomb had seared it like a burger on the grill. The lower portion of the thing's physique, everything below the neck, was totally normal, unscathed, as it had been standing behind a ten-foot-thick steel-and-stone barrier.

Only his head had been above the protection, only his head had received the full brunt of the rays, so that the flesh had burned and then melted, running in little rivers of red— the nose, the cheeks, the ears, all just sort of melting together. And when the dripping, oozing sores all had finally healed, this was what was left—just a mass of tissue like a bloody pudding that had been reassembled and then frozen into place. Stone stared into that gnarled face, that featureless visage, and saw the face of death. Knew that if death was going to take him—this was the form it would come in.

The faceless giant entered the cave and turned to Stone as the guards closed the bubble entrance behind it. He could just make out little blips of glistening tissue mushed into the center of the clay like tissue of the thing's eyes—like pencil dots behind burned eyelids and dripping brows. But nothing he could recognize as human stared back out.

"I'm going to make it more than fair," the Dwarf yelled out from the near table. "No weapons—just one man against another, hand to hand. The purest, most mythical of battles. You can go out in a blaze of glory, Stone. Have your name mumbled on the names of peasants until they die. And then you will be forgotten forever."

"Thanks," Stone screamed back. "I won't forget the favor."

"Ah, Stone," the Dwarf said appreciatively. "You're so combative, all the way to the end. That is why I have so enjoyed our intense but brief relationship. Good-bye, Mr. Stone. What is the sound of the end?" Dwarf paused dramatically, then, "It swallows its own scream—it makes no sound."

Stone heard a sound and shifted his attention completely back to the monstrosity with the melted face that came toward him now, crouched down like a cat. He had hoped, because of it tremendous size, that it must have outweighed him by a hundred and fifty pounds, that it would be clumsy and slow. But such was not to be the case. For the radiation-scarred mutilation circled around him, moving its hands in slow circles in the air, like a symphony conductor.

Suddenly, in a flash, the irradiated face was on him. Stone couldn't even see it coming, so fast did the attacker strike. But he sensed the attack, and instead of fighting it, went with the charge, falling backward on the floor and kicking up with his legs. The tree of muscle shot by overhead, launched by Stone's feet. It flew headfirst into the plastic wall and slid down in a heap. But by the time Stone had risen to his legs, the thing was standing too. It didn't even look fazed—just started forward again.

Stone decided to try boxing with the thing and began moving fast around it, making a circle to its left, as the thing appeared to be right-handed. He threw out fast jabs, punching with both hands at once since they were still cuffed together. It seemed to work at first. The thing was not used to the speed of a jab and took shot after shot to the face. Stone's hand sank into the squishy flesh, which almost seemed to come free around his hands like dough sticking to his fingers and wrist. But although he didn't even know what he was hitting, the thing didn't seem to like it and pulled back, raising it arms to cover its face. But Stone, a little overconfident, stepped forward to throw a right and suddenly, once again, the thing moved like lightning and was on him. He fell to the ground, the monstrous shape coming down right on top of him, and it began pounding his head into the floor over and over, like a coconut it was trying to break open. Its fighting techniques were of a basic nature.

Stone could feel his head about to open up and release its contents as everything filled with pain, the skull cracking against the hard floor. Above him he could see that swamp of a face, that thing that should exist only in a child's nightmare, peering down at him, as his head snapped up and down like a piston.

Somehow Stone reached inside himself for the strength for a final try and slammed both arms straight up. The fists missed each side of the melted face, but the cuffs in between hit the thing's throat, slamming so deeply into the flesh that blood immediately appeared in a band around the throat. Stone pulled his arm back, ready to strike again, but the thing was already gagging, rising to his feet, trying to breathe. He couldn't give it a second to recuperate. Though his head felt like it was coming off, though his eyes kept threatening not to focus, Stone knew that he couldn't stand a protracted battle with the thing. It was a hundred times stronger than him. It was now—now or never.

The melted face was already coming to its senses as Stone dragged himself to a standing position. The head was bearing around on him. Stone ran forward the three steps between them, and the thing grunted and raised its oak-log arms, closing them around Stone like the steel scoops of a steam shovel. But as they closed, Stone spun up with his entire body weight, bringing his right knee up into the thing's groin with the velocity and mass of a cannonball. The entire four hundred pounds of faceless muscle rose a good foot up into the air and let out a howl of unintelligible screams, bending over as if its stomach had been struck with a sledgehammer.

But Stone wasn't about to give the radiation-sculpted horror the standing eight count. As it came down hard, landing with its bare feet on the ground, he brought the knee up again and again into the thing's stomach, its groin, any damned thing he could find. And every time he struck, the faceless attacker just crouched more and more forward, as if frozen in paralysis. The face came down so low that Stone struck into that as well. The heavy bone of his kneecap just slammed into the formless flesh, rearranging it even more, as if anyone could notice. But the blows hit deeper, into the bones behind the plastic flesh. The face and cheek-bones shattered, and what was left of the nasal cartilage all splintered and drove back into the thing's brain.

Stone struck so many times, he lost count, driving the knee up until blood was spurting everywhere and he was covered with the stuff. At last he slipped in a puddle of red beneath his feet and fell down breathless, struggling backward along the floor, to get away from the thing if it attacked. But it was done for. Somehow it rose to its full height, whimpering and moaning like a dog in pain, and they could all see the extent of the injuries that Stone had inflicted on it. The knee had opened up the front of the skull so that it was nearly gone. The throbbing grapefruit-sized pink brain was clearly visible as it peered out from within the brain cavity, as if it were the new face, a replacement for the old shattered one.

Then the brain just seemed to slide out through the fissure of a face. Unattached to anything inside, as all the muscles had been turned to mush, the squirming brain gurgled out of the head and down the front of the bloody body. It landed on the floor and moved along it, leaving a slippery red trail behind it, until at last it crashed into the plastic wall and came to a stop, blood seeping out of it like an old sponge. The body, completely without brain, or much of anything above the neck, spasmed a few times and then crumpled straight down like a piece of rubber, the muscular arms and legs just seeming to whoosh out all their air and energy, so that the ugly thing almost seemed to deflate to half its size as it lay there oozing fluids from what had been its face.

CHAPTER
Twenty

"KILL HIM," Dwarf screamed from his dining table outside the bubble. He wriggled around furiously in the wheelchair as his stumps struggled to reach the firing buttons of the control panel on his side rest.

"Bastard, bastard, kill him!" the Dwarf screamed over and over again in that falsetto voice that Stone had come to hate so much. He dived for cover as he saw the blue-jumpsuited guards raising their tommy guns and sighting for his body. Stone came down hard on his stomach, landing just behind the brainless body that lay on the floor, still pumping liquid from the opened skull. Bullets poured into the side of the Plexiglas, some driving through and into the corpse barricade behind which Stone lay, trying to make himself flat against the floor.

But the slugs were edging closer, ripping into the floor with loud cracks as they poured in from every direction. It was only seconds before they dissected his backbone. Stone closed his eyes and waited for the end—at least it would be quick.

But as he starting wincing his eyes and gritting his teeth in anticipation of being ripped to shreds, there was a sudden tremendous roar that seemed to shake the whole floor. Stone tried to rise, but there was another, just as powerful, knocking him right back down.

He waited about ten seconds, hearing only screams and moans but no shots coming to take him out. The place was thick with smoke, and he edged carefully forward on hands and knees toward the entrance of the bubble. It was hard to tell what was happening. The smoke was still dense, and though he could see vague shapes yards off, everyone was just yelling incoherently. He had nothing to lose. Gathering all his strength, he breathed out and shot through the opening, his handcuffed fists ready to smash anything that came near. He had gone about fifteen feet toward what he thought was the main entrance when a shadow appeared out of nowhere just beyond the range of his vision and whispered sharply.

"Stone, Stone! Here man—here!" Stone pulled back the cuffed fists, ready to kill, and moved slowly forward one carefully placed foot at a time so he could swing out a kick with speed and power. The shape suddenly moved at him quickly, a scar-faced thug with black suit and feathered fedora. Stone had never seen the son of a bitch in his life. He wavered for a fraction of a second, debating whether to take the guy out when the face laughed.

"It's me Stone, don't you know? Kennedy. I saw you get popped at the slave auction, but I knew the Dwarf wouldn't be able to resist fucking with your head a little more. So I came in disguise—pretty good, heh?" He laughed again and suddenly fired the tommy gun he was holding just past Stone. A blue-jumpsuited guard went flying backward, as if a rocket were in his stomach.

"Let's get the fuck out of here," Stone spat as the smoke suddenly began clearing and dozens of the Mad army, along with the entire dinner party of gangsters and bikers, suddenly were staring at them, and every one of them was raising some kind of weapon.

"Immortal words," Kennedy said, pushing Stone forward, toward a curtain. As they ran, he heaved two metal balls over his shoulder, which went off as they hit the floor. Two smaller explosions again shook the place as clouds of foul-smelling smoke poured out in a flood.

"This way, this way," Kennedy kept yelling over his shoulder. "Hold you breath until we're out of here." But Stone didn't have to be told that, just the little traces of the smoke filtering in his nostrils made him want to vomit. The doc ran straight through the long purple curtain that covered the entire side of the room and through an open doorway into another room with four halls coming off it. Stone flew behind him like a tiger on his trail. Without hesitating, Kennedy took one of the hallways, and the two of them tore down it so fast that their boots and shoes were sliding crazily on the recently waxed tiles.

Ahead of them, two figures suddenly appeared far off, like ants down the yard-wide, brilliantly lit corridor.

"Stop," one of them yelled, holding his arm up and advancing on the two men.

"Stop, my asshole," Kennedy muttered to Stone, and opened up with the smg, swinging it back and forth so slugs pinged down the hallway in a maelstrom of spinning lead. The ants crumbled, their forms spitting red. The two fleeing men ran right over them, jumping on their bodies to get over the puddles of blood, like leaping rocks on a stream. Without breaking stride, Stone grabbed one of the dead guard's submachine guns and two magazines of ammo and swung it up, aiming straight ahead. Now he felt just a little better. At the end of the corridor, Kennedy tore through the door to the left and pulled Stone in, slamming the door behind them. They both leaned against the wall in the darkened supply closet, breathing heavily.

"Where the hell are we going?" Stone asked, wondering if the snake doctor had the slightest idea of how to get out. "This place is like a maze." He looked around at the plentitude of mops, brooms, and buckets that filled the small room.

"I got the plans, pal," Kennedy said, tapping his fingers against his head. He looked so different, it amazed Stone. Scars along both cheeks, thick eyebrows; his goatee seemed completely gone, turning into a patch of dark, fuzzy mustache that saddled the top lip. "Always use your head first. It's amazing how many people don't follow that simple advice. See—I got the architectural plans for the building. I won't even tell you how easy they were to snatch. No one even thought to protect them. They'll be looking for us on all the main halls and stairwells. They won't come this way for at least a few minutes. But according to these plans"— he took out a miniature flashlight hardly larger than a cigarette and shone it on the crumbling, blue-lined drawings—"there's an old pulley system in these walls. Used to be used to pick up and deliver laundry from floor to floor. Let's see, should be right—" He stopped and banged against what seemed to be solid wall. And it was. He tried again a foot away, and Stone joined in, both of them banging on the wall a little anxiously. At last, near the very corner, Stone felt a little give, and the faintest echoing sound from the other side.

He reached around, grabbed a shovel, and, pulling back, smashed into the green-painted surface with all his strength. Half the wall came tumbling down over them as they were inundated with broken plaster and a cloud of dust. They looked at each other as Kennedy held his flashlight up through the cloud—they looked terrible, so covered with grit that they both appeared to be in blackface, ready to break into dance.

"It's true," Kennedy said as he stepped through the settling dust and into a square shaftway on the other side. Stone came through alongside him, and the two men looked up. It was just about pitch-black, except far up at the very top where there must have been some sort of vent or opening, for they could see a dim pencil dot of light. Stone reached out and grabbed hold of a thick rope that came down from out of the darkness.

"This is it—the beanstalk," Stone said, shaking the thing and pulling on it to see if it was still functional.

"It will take us to the Dwarf, Stone—and probably your sister. I overheard one of his personal elite guards. His suite is on the eighteenth level—the entire level—and there was a woman there. A special one that the Dwarf apparently had special plans for."

"Jesus." Stone's face went white, even in the darkness. "It's her, I know it. We've got to, got to—"

"Slow down, slow down," Kennedy said, reaching out for the rope. "We got a long climb ahead. You're going to need every fucking bit of strength you got!"

They climbed for what seemed like hours. At first they moved fast, especially Stone. But the rope was so old that, although in no danger of snapping because of its thickness, the fibers came off in their hands, itching them, grinding into them, making their fingers and palms swell up red. And with no ventilation whatsoever in the shaft—and virtually no air, either—it was like breathing on the summit of Mt. Everest. Slowly they dragged themselves on. Both knew there was no going down, so it wasn't a question of that, just of pushing their bodies and lungs to the absolute limits of their endurance. They climbed a yard, two yards, then stopped. A foot, two feet. Stop. They would rest by wrapping their feet around the rope or by stepping on the ledges that came out of the sealed-up laundry holes.

Kennedy kept careful track of each landing as they passed. And finally they were there. They both came right up to the floor, resting their feet on the metal shelf.

"Are the old laundry drops all in supply rooms?" Stone whispered to Kennedy, in case there was someone just on the other side of the wall.

"That's what they tell me," he replied, scanning the blueprints once again with a quick wave of the flashlight.

"Well, there's no time like the present," Stone grunted,

and pulling back, he slammed the butt of the tommy gun into the wall. It cracked on the first strike, opened up a hole on the second hit, and by the fifth was already crumbling into a space large enough for them to squeeze through. It was a supply room. Stone tiptoed to the door and put his ear to it. He could hear sounds far off, but nothing that sounded remotely close. Certainly nothing right outside the door. He motioned for Kennedy to come behind him and put his fingers over his lips. They'd keep it quiet for as long as they could.

He pulled open the door with a quick yank and stepped out into the bright corridor, turning both ways in a fraction of a second, the smg held high. To his surprise, one of the blue-jumpsuited guards was sitting just feet from the supply room, leaning back in a chair, reading a magazine. The man's face registered fear, shock, amazement, horror— every damned thing that a man feels in the space of one second when he knows he's about to die. He moved his weight forward and came down on the chair, reaching for his tommy gun lying against the wall. But he didn't have a chance. As the man's head came down, Stone rushed forward and slammed the stock of the smg right up into the softest part of the throat and the underside of the jaw.

The guard stood straight up, his face bright red, and though he tried to scream, he could only gurgle and spit out little gobs of blood as he sort of jumped up and down on his toes, as if doing an odd form of calisthentics. Stone and Kennedy rushed past the dying guard, not even bothering to finish him off. The walking corpse wouldn't get three feet. They tore ass down the corridor. Now the only problem was to find the quadriplegic warlord.

Suddenly Kennedy stopped and grabbed Stone by the shoulder, putting his finger over his lips. They both listened in the brilliant illumination of the hall—and heard it—far-off, deep chanting, singing of some kind. Like monks chanting on a far mountain. They started running again and stopped when they came to an intersection of three halls, listening again. Thus they followed the sound for several minutes, winding through the myriad passageways of the resort. The closer they got, the stranger and more unpleasant the chanting became. It was dark, like some Gregorian chant of death from the Middle Ages. Like a song celebrating death and plague and rats, rather than life and spirit. The voices seemed to cry rather than sing, moaning out unintelligible lyrics of torture and despair.

"Sounds like there's a lot of them," Kennedy said as they came to a corner. He peered around—there was a wide set of wooden doors about thirty feet away and two guards standing in front of it. The ritual, or whatever it was, was clearly going on just behind the doors.

"I want to get in there quietly," Stone said, his eyes taking on a more and more wild look as they grew closer to April and the hell she might be undergoing at this very instant. "We've got to get in there before they hear us."

"I think I know how," the snake man said, reaching into his wide, double-breasted jacket and pulling out one of the smoke bombs he had been carrying. He threw it to the floor just their side of the corner, and a plume of smoke came out, this one not as large as the ones in the dining room and without the terrible smell. But it did the trick. The guards came running the moment they saw the smoke, both totally forgetting their duties, even dropping their weapons by the door. They flew around the corridor, and two smg stocks smashed into both their faces so hard that they were both stock-dead and crashed onto the floor with heavy thuds.

Stone and Kennedy flew toward the door. The chanting was loud, very loud, and rising to some kind of crescendo, as if something bad was about to happen. Kennedy glanced at Stone to plan their entrance, but Stone was beyond all that. With a look of animal ferocity on his face he rushed shoulder first toward the wooden doors with the full weight of his body. The doors flew open and Stone fell forward, slipping and rolling on the ground for a second. He came up on one knee and whipped the smg to chest level and stared straight ahead. And what he saw was the most horrible thing he had ever seen in his life.

For hanging on a double-crosspieced crucifix, the same kind that the Brotherhood of the Same had used in Pueblo, was Stone's sister April. And she was nailed to it. Huge penny nails through both hands, which dripped little trickles of blood. Her head just swung back and forth, the mouth only able to issue forth with little moans. She had stopped screaming hours before. All around the Dwarf were his chorus of black-robed death worshipers, their mouths opened in mid-chant as they stared at the man staring wildly back at them.

"It's our way of celebrating Christmas," the Dwarf hissed at Stone. "*Our* Christmas."

"Bastard," Stone spat out, his voice like the side of a

razor blade. "Bastard, bastard!" He jumped to his feet, standing feet apart, put his hand on the trigger, and just pulled. He swung the trembling tommy gun, which sprayed wildly weaving .45 slugs like there was no tomorrow. He held the trigger until the last bullet was gone and then slammed another magazine into the thing and fired again, until every black-robed shape in front of him was motionless, covered with oozing red dots that contrasted sharply against the dark black of their robes.

Stone, fighting back tears but failing, ran toward April, whose own eyes were open now, and wet, as she saw him, saw her brother, who she had prayed—since the day she was captured—would save her. It was all that had kept her going, the only thing. Otherwise she would have committed suicide long before. And so, even though in intense pain, she smiled the softest of smiles at him as he rushed to her.

"God God," Stone said over and over again as he heard scuffling off to the side and saw Kennedy kicking the Dwarf-thing from its chair so that it lay squirming on the floor, shaking itself from side to side, like a snake without coils, a turtle on its back, a slug that couldn't move an inch. But Stone didn't even hear it. He reached up and, gripping his hand around one of the nails that protruded from her hand, pulled it with all his might. Slowly it came free. Then the other. He didn't even notice the deep gouges in his palms and on the insides of his fingers that filled with blood. He caught her in his arms as she fell. She looked so vulnerable, so young and innocent, almost as she had been when she was a little girl. And again the tears filled his eyes, and this time, against anything his will could do, they fell.

He placed her gently on the floor, grabbing one of the nearby robes and ripping it from its occupant, who didn't need it any longer. She was wearing the same skimpy burlap bag of a miniskirt that all the slavewhores wore, and she seemed cold, shivering. He covered her and just held her head in his hands, stroking her hair.

"It's okay now, baby. It's all over. You're okay. I'll take you home—and you'll be okay. I'm sure. Everything will be okay."

She opened her eyes and somehow managed to move her parched lips. "Okay, okay. Is that all you know how to say?"

"Oh, April," he said, hugging her, knowing that if she could insult him, she would live. He lay her down again and turned to see what was happening behind him. They were all dead. Every one of them. Only Dwarf himself had survived, by swinging his wheelchair around, protected by its bulletproof back. Now he just lay there, like a diseased thing rolling wildly on its round stomach as it looked up at Stone, shaking its pasty, pin-eyed head.

"You can't kill me, Stone. I am the death nature, the energy that is the true base of humanity. I am stronger than you. Always and forever. You can't kill me."

The words were too much for Stone. After everything, they were just too much. He walked over to the slithering, stumped thing and lifted it up by the back of its own black robe, making sure he didn't actually touch its flesh. The idea nauseated him. Like touching the foul excrement of a bat, the pus of a leper. The very nearness of the Dwarf made him shiver violently, his skin crawling as if the roaches were on him again. He headed toward the window as the thing pulled wildly in all directions, trying to hit futilely at him with its stumps, kicking with its mushroom-shaped feet. He walked to the window, opened it wide, and pulling back the murderous ball of destruction, he heaved it forward with all his strength into the air.

It gave Stone the greatest satisfaction to see the misshapen flesh spin off into the darkness as Dwarf's high-pitched screams quickly vanished in the mist. He turned back from the window.

"Well done, lad," Kennedy said. "Well done."

The Dwarf spun end over end like a meteor, building up speed fast, as he didn't even have the arms or legs to create friction. The world whirled around him in a kaleidoscope of color and light, and the air moved so fast, he could hardly breathe. He screamed, his voice just making an animal sound. It couldn't be—not he—not the Dwarf. He was . . . immortal. He couldn't die. Couldn't! But as he saw the ground suddenly coming up at him like a fist, he knew that he could. He hit and felt a terrible ripping and suffocating sensation. But he didn't die. Kept going down, down, a terrible pressure building up around his head and body. The pool—frozen for winter ice skating. He had cracked through the thin ice and was in the water. He was alive. He was alive. Freezing and in tremendous pain, feeling as if every organ in his body had been smashed to pulp, the Dwarf somehow managed to hold his breath as he slowly rose to the surface where he bobbed like a cork, too mean to sink.

CHAPTER
Twenty-one

"WE'VE GOT to move," Kennedy said, looking down at Stone, who had bandaged April's hands and was holding a glass of water, which she slowly drank down.

"Impossible," Stone said. "Look at her."

"Have to, pal," Kennedy repeated. "They'll be here soon—real soon. None of us will be any good dead. Can you move at all, April?" Kennedy asked, getting down on one knee.

"Imposs—" Stone started to say again, this time louder and angrier.

"Quiet, Martin," the prone girl said in a whisper. "I can move. I look worse than I think I really am. Other than the nails in my hand, he was mostly humiliating me by things he said and poking around my body with a stick on the end of his wheelchair. But I'll live. Help me up," she said, and as Stone looked down at her as if she were crazy, she said it again. "I said help me up, goddammit, I'm not a cripple."

Her words shocked Stone so much that he stood up, and she rose with him. She put her hand to her face and almost seemed to swoon for a second but then straightened up as both men started toward her, holding her hand up to stop them.

"I don't feel great, but I can function. A little," she added softly.

"Okay, this is it," Kennedy said quickly to Stone. "We head to the back—I know the way—and go out by way of the mountain, not the building. We'll never get out of here, but straight down the side a few hundred yards to the side in the darkness, they'll never see us."

"Look, Kennedy, don't be ridiculous—she might be able to walk, but she sure as hell can't climb down the side of a goddamned mountain," Stone said, looking at his sister, whom he wanted to grab and hold up, so delicate and frail did she look. But he knew she would just get furious and push him away. Suddenly he felt a surge of love for her, more perhaps than he had ever felt when they had just been residents of the same house, trying to stay out of each other's way. She was stubborn—and tough. Tough as hell. Like him.

"It's the only way. I'm a good climber—excellent, for that matter—and I just happen to have..." He pulled out a tightly wrapped coil of what looked like thin cord on a plastic spool from a bag he had thrown around his shoulder. "We'll tie her to my back and I'll take her down. You cover from behind. It will scare the shit out of her, but I doubt anything can be worse than what she's already gone through."

Stone looked away, thought for a moment, and then turned back.

"Let's go," he said.

When they got to the back part of the floor, Kennedy led them out to a terrace and then to the end of it and right out onto the side of the mountain into which the huge resort had been built. It looked like it dropped down forever, with jagged edges looming out of the darkness.

"Here, help me strap her on," Kennedy said as he handed Stone a mini-harness with three straps. Stone attached the nylon-webbed straps around her chest and under her arms and then clicked them into some snap latches on a similar arrangement Kennedy had strapped to himself.

"There, tight as two butterflies in a cocoon," Kennedy said, trying to break the tension. But both Stone and his sister had greenish skin color. "Now we just attach this here," Kennedy said, snapping one end of the cord to a thick steel fence cemented deep into the side of the terrace. "And"—he threw the spool far over the side so that it unraveled, shooting down into the darkness of the rocks below—"voilà, instant escape. Here, you might need these." He handed Stone the pack, containing a number of grenadelike devices. "The ones with red tape are smoke; with blue, explosive. Pull the lever on the side and throw. Easier than boiling eggs."

"This rope looks like string," Stone said as he ran his fingers over it, visualizing his sister spinning in the darkness the way the dwarf had.

"Tested to a thousand pounds, my friend, I promise you," Kennedy said as he stepped over the side and placed one foot on the crumbling side of the cliff. "Anyway, I'll find out. See you down below." With that, he pushed up and careened far out into the air, away from the mountain, so that Stone could hear April gasp. Then they were gone into the shadows below, and Stone couldn't see a trace of them.

Suddenly Stone heard the sound of glass breaking and turned around, startled. Somehow he hadn't been thinking they were coming yet. An almost fatal mistake. A hail of slugs came toward him, screaming out his name. Stone threw himself back against the cliff wall, and the bullets dug into the rock just inches away, filling the air with a storm of particles. The firing kept up for what seemed a minute, with Stone hugged to the wall, not moving an inch, not even breathing.

The second he heard it slacken and voices start, Stone grabbed two of the exploding pineapples and pulled them, jumping forward and throwing them both simultaneously. Just as quickly he dived below the edge of the terrace. Screams, and then boots running on rock. But just for a second. Then the eggs went off with the roar of artillery shells, and there were more screams. Without waiting for the smoke to clear, Stone stepped forward, took another, and threw it. He dove down, waited for the explosion, walked forward twenty feet through the smoking bodies and the blood, and threw another. It wasn't a night for strategy— just pure, quick death as fiery ball after fiery ball erupted and ripped into everything around it. Thus did Martin Stone move forward across the terrace, blasting his way through scores of the Dwarf's private army, leaving them as disassembled pieces swimming in their own blood.

Seeing no one shooting at him—at that instant, any-way—just a long, flat outcropping filled with human parts, Stone took out two of the grenades, armed them, dropped them back in the sack, and threw the whole package with all his strength so that it flew through the air nearly ninety feet straight up, slamming into the side of the mountain above. He dived forward, just getting inside the door, and scrambled ahead. Behind him the slope erupted and came crashing down, taking the terrace with it as a whole section of the upper left part of the resort tumbled down the side of the mountain. A cloud of dust rose and ballooned into the room where Stone lay. He jumped to his feet, swinging the tommy gun around from behind his back and ran forward into the semidarkness, not even knowing where he was going. He kicked through a door and into a corridor where five of the blue-ski-parkaed guards walking about thirty feet away stopped and began to turn.

Stone opened up with the smg, spraying it as he walked forward. More appeared, but he just kept firing, walking rapidly down the hallway, not even taking his finger from the trigger. They fell before him like bleeding bowling pins as the half-crazed man, cut and bleeding in a thousand places, covered from head to toe in dust and grit, his teeth grinding together like unoiled gears, exterminated them. He never stopped firing, holding the tommy gun in one arm, finger on the trigger until it was empty, then slamming in another mag, of which there were plenty to grab lying along the hall next to their dead owners.

Stone shot a half load through a door and then followed behind, kicking it open. But those who had been waiting behind it were just holes now, holes with dying flesh around them. He was in the inner courtyard near the highest level, and he could see the partying masses of sick souls far below. This whole place had to go. Now. He had cut off the bastards from getting access to Kennedy or April. They'd get away. And Stone? Stone would do what had to be done. Somehow, with all the excitement, he managed to get all the way to the elevator banks without encountering any opposition. He pushed the button of one of ten elevators, and at last it banged open. Two guards were inside talking to one another, and Stone came in, smg talking death. The door closed behind him, and two bodies slid to the floor leaving long, smeared trails of red on the chromium walls behind them.

Stone pressed the "subbasement" button, and the elevator slowly headed down outside the huge resort. As he neared the ground level someone glanced up and saw him standing with the smg in arms and the two bloody bodies behind him. A woman screamed. And then shots rang out. But Stone was already sinking through the main level, disappearing down into the earth.

The doors flew open, and he shot out into the immense open floor that spread out as far as he could see. Machines chugged, and steam seemed to rise up out of every crevice. The air was thick, and Stone started sweating almost immediately. He headed into the steaming mists, feeling as if he were strolling through a primeval forest. It must have been a hunderd and twenty degrees—and getting hotter as he walked forward. Huge generators turned in a blur, powered by immense diesel engines that had been rigged up below. The Resort's power supply. And far across the room

Stone saw something that made his eyes open wide. Four immense tanks, each sixty feet long and ten in diameter. And he knew what was in them.

He started forward between the generators when a technician suddenly came down a ladder and stared at him. The man went for a pistol strapped on his hip. But Stone brought up the muzzle of the tommy gun and slammed the tip into the man's fat stomach. He pulled the trigger for a few seconds. The whole middle of the man just sort of disintegrated, and Stone stepped back, giving it room to splatter onto the floor. He ran over to the tanks and saw that they had nozzles on one end controlled by big, hand-turned wheels above them. Stone stopped for a second and closed his eyes. He knew once he moved he couldn't stop moving. Couldn't slow down for a second—or he was dead. In his mind he visualized where he would run, how he would try to make his escape. The Major had always told him that. "Picture your escape route before you attack, then even when you become disoriented, confused, you'll still instinctively know how to get out."

He reached forward, turning the first of the metal wheels. It seemed to stick at first but then went. He twisted it fast and it spun open, a torrent of gasoline suddenly pouring out on the ground, rushing around his feet. Stone ran to each of the others, doing the same, and then tore back toward the elevator, a whole section of the floor already filled with a spreading puddle. Things were moving a little faster than he'd planned, Stone suddenly realized as he pressed the elevator button and waited. The generators were only about fifty yards off from the petrol ocean. Once they met...

"Fuck it." He scanned the walls and saw the fire exit, running toward it and slamming the steel door open against the inside wall. He took the stairs three at a time and tore up the two flights to the main level. He came to a steel door marked LOBBY and flung it open, coming out firing, not caring what the hell he hit. A crowd of bikers were walking by, and the slugs scattered them to the ground like so many broken branches from a storm. Stone ran past them and down the courtyard as screams echoed from behind him and shots rang out, one whizzing just past his ear. He saw a big Mack truck just driving into the main court, and from the faces peering through the side vents, he could see that they were girls—more whores and slaves to feed to Dwarf's perverted hordes. But not tonight.

He felt something dig into his calf but was already running toward the truck that had just pulled to a stop next to a loading dock. Stone reached the door just as the driver was getting down and grabbed hold of the jacket's lapel, pulling down with all his strength. The slave trucker slammed down into the hard stone street without even a chance to protect himself, his face evening out to fit better with the hard surface it met. Stone jumped up into the seat and saw the keys still hanging in the ignition, the engine on.

"What the hell's going on?" a face yelled out, pressing up against a grating that led to the back of the truck.

"We're going for a ride," Stone yelled through the side of his mouth without turning around. "Tell the ladies back there to all lie down and get ready to crash." Stone put the tommy gun up on the dashboard and started the huge vehicle forward. He had trouble with the complicated gearshift, and the thing jerked ahead, lurching forward and backward so that the wheels lifted slightly off the ground. But once he got it going, he didn't stop. The truck careened down the courtyard and out to the main tunnel. The guards at the checkpoint already had their metal gate down and their weapons drawn, all of them sighting on the windshield. Stone aimed the smg through the window, ducked his head down, and pulled the trigger, holding it for three seconds, and then brought his head up again.

He was almost on the gate, two of the guards already twitching in their private swimming pools. The third stood there firing at the truck, frozen, as if hypnotized by the roaring vehicle.

"Bye-bye, buddy," Stone said as he shifted up another gear and floored it. The diesel rocketed ahead, slamming into the guard and grinding him beneath its churning wheels, depositing him out the back, more putty than flesh. The Mack truck slammed through the two-inch steel pole like it was a toothpick and hurtled forward into the tunnel that led outside. He prayed there was no incoming traffic—or they were all going to spend a long, long time in intimate contact with one another. But the truck met only whistling air as it streamed through the tunnel. He could see the other end just fifty yards off, and the outer guard post with another pole and more men wanting to be turned into jam. Stone would oblige them.

The truck barreled through the tunnel at increasing acceleration, heaving back and forth so that occasionally one of the sides scraped against a wall and Stone could hear a chorus of screams from the back. But the thing just surged ahead by sheer kinetic energy and sped out of the other end like a missile leaving its silo.

Then everything happened at once. The guards firing, the truck driving over them, making their faces vanish from sight. They were just outside the end of the tunnel, into the air, when it went. The whole damned resort. Stone could feel the shock waves rippling through the ground, shock waves that seemed to lift the whole truck in the air. Then the light that filled the sky behind him and overhead with the brilliance of a midday sun. Then the sound, as if he were standing dead center of an A-bomb. There was another roar just as loud and the sound of something avalanching, falling on them. Stone floored the Mack, leaning forward like a jockey on a mount, trying to urge the truck on.

There was a sound like rain—but much louder—and he saw a small shower of pebbles landing on the windshield and the hood. The pebbles got bigger, and the whole truck began vibrating and slowing, sounding as if artillery shells were falling on every square inch of it. Then the windshield in front of him went totally black, and Stone felt an incredible pressure on his head and chest, as if he were being squashed, suffocated, crushed into nothingness.

CHAPTER
Twenty-two

H E HEARD digging, scraping sounds. Then there was light. He opened his eyes as hands reached down for him and pulled him up from the wreckage. Women—the women from the truck—cut and bleeding, nearly fifty of them. They all stood around the pile of rubble that had buried the truck. Behind them, on the other side of the ridge through which the tunnel had once snaked before it collapsed into dust, the sky was still filled with fire, softer now but glowing, as if it would burn forever.

One of the whores helped Stone sit up next to her on a large chunk of porous rock that had slammed in the top of the driver's cabin, nearly crushing Stone to something that could be spread on a sandwich.

"I saved you because I figure you saved us, right?" the whore asked. She was a tough old thing, like the meanest old sow of the barnyard, with acne scars beneath her powdered cheeks, a few teeth missing, and the edge of a tattoo showing here and there. She sat, nearly naked in the few tatters that were left of her clothes, with the muscles of a man on her thick arms.

"Yeah, that's right," Stone said, touching his right shoulder, which almost felt broken, along with every other goddamned part of him. "I saved you."

"What the hell happened in there?" she asked, looking incredulously up at the towering ball of oil smoke that seemed to rise all the way into the clouds where it mixed with them, turning the heavens into a churning sea of black.

"I think they had a boiler problem," Stone muttered, unable to meet her ancient, dead eyes. He tried to stand up and felt his ankle almost give, but he moved his boot to a different angle and forced the damned ankle to hold him whether it wanted to or not.

From the top of the rubble where he stood he could see the very top of the Resort, or what had been the top. The whole thing was gone now. Just the raw face of a mountain that had the whole front of it ripped free. A lot of evil had been buried in that burning rubble, he thought, his eyes reflecting the flames like mirrors. Maybe he had actually done something good for this fucked-up wreck of a world. Not that it had a chance of surviving. But if it did—if somehow it did—maybe he had pushed the scales of darkness and light, death and life, to the side of the living. Just a little.

Now all he had to do was fix his broken shoulder, find April and Kennedy, and then get back to the damned dog, waiting with its accusing eyes out there in the middle of nowhere. Why, there was nothing to it. He'd get moving in one second. As soon as he caught his breath.

MORE FROM QUESTAR®...

THE BEST IN SCIENCE FICTION AND FANTASY

___**FORBIDDEN WORLD**   *(E20-017, $2.95, U.S.A.)*
by David R. Bischoff and Ted White   *(E20-018, $3.75, Canada)*

This is a novel about a distant world designed as a social experiment. Forbidden World recreates regency London, Rome in the time of the Caesars, and a matriarchal agrarian community in a distant part of space—with devastating results!

___**THE HELMSMAN**   *(E20-027, $2.95, U.S.A.)*
by Merl Baldwin   *(E20-026, $3.75, Canada)*

A first novel that traces the rise of Wilf Brim, a brash young starship cadet and son of poor miners, as he tries to break the ranks of the aristocratic officers who make up the Imperial Fleet—and avenge the Cloud League's slaughter of his family.

___**THE HAMMER AND THE HORN**   *(E20-028, $2.95, U.S.A.)*
by Michael Jan Friedman   *(E20-029, $3.75, Canada)*

Taking its inspiration from Norse mythology, this first novel tells the story of Vidar, who fled Asgard for Earth after Ragnarok, but who now must return to battle in order to save both worlds from destruction.

27 million Americans can't read a bedtime story to a child.

It's because 27 million adults in this country simply can't read.

Functional illiteracy has reached one out of five Americans. It robs them of even the simplest of human pleasures, like reading a fairy tale to a child.

You can change all this by joining the fight against illiteracy.

Call the Coalition for Literacy at toll-free **1-800-228-8813** and volunteer.

Volunteer Against Illiteracy. The only degree you need is a degree of caring.

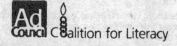

Ad Council Coalition for Literacy

Warner Books is proud to be an active supporter of the Coalition for Literacy.